THE CORPORATE BRIDEGROOM

BY

LIZ FIELDING

MILLS & BOON®

First published in Great Britain 2001
Large Print edition 2002
Harlequin Mills & Boon Limited,
Eton House, 18-24 Paradise Road,
Richmond, Surrey TW9 1SR

© Liz Fielding 2002

ISBN 0 263 17357 7

Set in Times Roman 16½ on 18½ pt.
16-0902-47561

Printed and bound in Great Britain
by Antony Rowe Ltd, Chippenham, Wiltshire

THE CORPORATE
BRIDEGROOM

PROLOGUE

PRESS RELEASE

CLAIBOURNE & FARRADAY are pleased to announce that Miss India Claibourne is to be appointed Managing Director with immediate effect.

Miss Romana Claibourne and Miss Flora Claibourne have been appointed full board members.

CITY DIARY, LONDON EVENING POST

Has sexual equality finally penetrated the hallowed portals of London's oldest and most stylish department store?

With today's announcement that India Claibourne, 29, is to step into her father's shoes as Managing Director of Claibourne & Farraday, an era ends as one of the last bastions of male domination is finally breached.

It seems the gorgeous Claibourne girls, who have been part of the management team since they were old enough to dress up as elves and help Santa in his grotto, have decided it's time to put an end to the nineteenth century male imperialism of the founders.

Not since 1832, when C&F founders, valet Charles Claibourne and butler William Farraday, hammered out an agreement of succession that hands a 'golden share' and total control to the oldest male heir of either family, has their authority been challenged.

Will the Farraday men take this lying down? Watch this space.

MEMORANDUM
From: JORDAN FARRADAY
To: NIALL FARRADAY MACAULAY
BRAM FARRADAY GIFFORD

I'm sure you've already seen the attached newspaper clipping. To answer any questions you may have, I have issued an immediate legal challenge to India Claibourne's position as Managing Director.

The Claibourne response is interesting. They have not, as I had expected, taken the feminist stance, or fallen back on sexual equality legislation. They instead evinced surprise that three such 'busy men could find the time to assume day-to-day running of a 'retail outlet'.

It is possible that they suspect it is our intention to liquidise the considerable assets in the C&F trademark and property and sell out which, once we gain control, they will be powerless to prevent. They must be convinced otherwise, which is why I have agreed to the suggestion that we each spend some time work-shadowing them during the next three months.

The Claibournes apparently hope to demonstrate that their 'hands-on' experience is a greater asset to Claibourne & Farraday than our years in the City. A delay of three months in the spirit of co-operation will do us no harm if, as I suspect it will, this ends up in court. The inside knowledge gained will serve us well if we have to go to court in order to evict them from the boardroom.

The timetable I've agreed is that Niall will shadow Romana Claibourne during April, Bram will do the same with Florence Claibourne during May, and I will work with India during June. I attach a dossier on each of your respective partners for you to study. Please give as much time as you can spare to this project without it appearing to intrude on your normal activities.

I realise this is an imposition but, as joint shareholders, I ask you to remember that the reward will be total control of a prime retail investment and one of the most valuable pieces of real estate in the country.

EMAIL
To: Romana@Claibournes.com
cc: Flora@Claibournes.com
From: India
Claibournes.com
Subject: Niall Farraday Macaulay
Romana

The lawyers have asked for three months to come up with a rebuttal of the Farraday claim to run Claibournes. As a delaying tactic I've had to 'play nice' and offer the Farradays an opportunity to see how we run Claibourne's—from the inside.

Niall Farraday Macaulay will be contacting you shortly to arrange a convenient schedule for him to shadow you during April. The man is an investment banker and would, no doubt, love a chance to get his hands on the Claibourne & Farraday assets. I need you to convince him that it's in *his* best interests to leave them with us.

That the Farradays accepted an invitation to shadow our roles in the company suggests they see it as an information-gathering opportunity. Please be on your guard.

Indie

CHAPTER ONE

ROMANA CLAIBOURNE, juggling a desperately needed carton of her favourite coffee, a small leather overnight bag and a couple of designer carrier bags, searched her handbag for her wallet in a state of rising panic. Not that the panic was entirely due to her missing wallet, or even Niall Farraday Macauley's annoying decision to make his presence felt on today of all days.

In spite of anything her sister might believe, there were worse things in the world than men with Farraday in their name.

Worse even than being late.

That was nothing new—she'd never been early for anything. Yet India's crisp little voice mail message this morning had been very clear on one point. Punctuality was essential. Niall Macaulay wanted to discuss shadowing arrangements with her at twelve o'clock sharp and she was to drop everything and be on time.

Nothing—not even the opening event in Claibourne & Farraday's annual charity week—was more important. This was a *crisis*.

And this was the good part of her day.

'Sorry…' She threw an apologetic glance at the cab driver. 'I know it's in here somewhere. I had it when I picked up—'

'In your own time, miss,' the man replied, cutting her short. 'I've got all day.'

She glanced up. 'Have you?' Then, realising he was being sarcastic, she pulled a face and redoubled her efforts to find the elusive wallet. She knew she'd had it when she picked up her dress because she'd used her charge card. Then, after she'd got India's message, coffee had seemed essential and she'd needed change to pay for it.

She re-ran the scene in her head. She'd ordered, paid and stuffed the wallet into her pocket…

Her relief was short-lived.

Reaching into the depths of her coat was just one stretch too far and the coffee-carton made an escape bid.

Hitting the pavement, it bounced, spun and then the lid flew off, releasing a hot tide of *latte*. Romana watched as in what seemed like slow-motion it washed over the gleaming, handmade shoes of a passing male before splashing spectacularly up the legs of his trousers.

The shoes, and the legs, came to a halt. The carton was picked up on the point of a furled silk black umbrella and she followed its progress until it came to a stop six inches from the second button of her coat.

'Yours, I believe,' the owner of the trousers said.

She took the carton. A mistake. It was now wet and sticky and the apology which had leapt instantly to her lips transformed itself into a disgusted, *'Eeeugh.'*

And then—mistake number two—she looked up and nearly dropped the carton again. He was everything a tall, dark stranger could and should be, and for a moment she froze, quite literally lost for words. Apologise. She must apologise. And find out who he was.

Even as she opened her mouth she realised that he was far from being impressed by his unexpected encounter with one of the most sought-after women in London. The man's expression encompassed entire sections of the thesaurus, involving the words ''stupid'', ''blonde'' and ''woman'', and the apology died on her lips.

It didn't matter. He clearly wasn't interested in anything she might have to say. He had already turned and was walking quickly through the gilded portal of Claibourne & Farraday, leaving her on the pavement with her mouth still open.

Niall Macaulay was expected, and was whisked up to the penthouse office suite where he handed his coat and umbrella to the receptionist before retreating to the cloakroom to wipe the coffee off his trousers and shoes. Tossing the paper towel in the bin, he glanced at his wrist-watch with irritation. He'd had scarcely enough time to make this appointment, and now that stupid woman had made him late.

What on earth had she been doing, juggling a carton of coffee with enough designer bags to keep a small country out of debt? She couldn't even control her hair.

But it didn't matter. Romana Claibourne was late, too. He declined her secretary's offer of coffee, accepted her invitation to wait in Miss Claibourne's opulent office and crossed to the window, trying not to dwell on a dozen other, more important things he should be doing at that moment.

'Not your day, miss, is it?' the cabby remarked as Romana continued to stare after the man. What a grouch... 'Do you want a receipt?'

'What? Oh, yes. Here—' She handed the man a banknote. 'Keep the change.'

She was still holding the dripping carton. There were no rubbish bins in the street and she was forced to carry the thing at arm's length up to her office.

Her secretary relieved her of the carton, took her bags and her coat. 'I'm expecting a Mr Macaulay. I can't spare him more than five minutes so I'm counting on you to rescue me…' she began, then caught the girl's warning look.

'Mr Macauley arrived a couple of minutes ago, Romana,' she murmured. 'He's waiting in your office.'

She spun around and saw a man standing at the window, looking out across the rooftops of London. Oh, knickers! He must have heard her. Great start. She grabbed a tissue, wiped her hands, and abandoned any thought of lipstick repair or getting her hair under control— but then there wasn't enough time in the world for that. She just smoothed her skirt, tugged her jacket into place and stepped into her office.

Niall Macauley was impressive, at least from the rear. Tall, with perfectly groomed dark hair, and a suit in which every stitch had been placed by hand expensively covering his broad shoulders.

'Mr Macaulay?' she said, crossing the office, hand extended in welcome as he turned. 'I'm so sorry to have kept you waiting.' About to explain her lateness—without mentioning coffee—she discovered that her legitimate excuses were redundant and instead found her mouth gaping like a surprised goldfish as he turned to her and took her hand.

There was, she thought, an almost Gothic inevitability that Niall Macaulay and the grouch she'd drowned with her coffee should be the same person. It was, after all, the first of April. All Fools' Day.

'Did my secretary offer you…?'

'Coffee?' he completed for her when she faltered. He spoke in a deep bass voice that she knew, just knew, would never be raised above that quiet, controlled level. No matter how provoked. She'd already had an example of his exceptional powers of self-control. 'Thank you, but I believe I've had all the coffee I can handle from you for one day.' As he released her hand, it seemed to Romana that there was just a hint of stickiness.

And the word 'crisis' took on a new depth of meaning.

This man was one of their 'silent' partners? It had never occurred to her to wonder, until recently, why they *were* so silent when their name was over the front door. If she'd thought about them at all, she'd assumed they were too old, or maybe just not interested in working when the dividends from the Claibourne family's industry was more than adequate to sustain three averagely lazy millionaires.

It was only after their father's near fatal heart attack that she and her sisters had discovered the truth. That, far from being sedentary, their partners—the venture capitalist, the banker and the lawyer—were empire-building on their own account.

And now they wanted the Claibourne empire too.

This was the banker. A man who'd already demonstrated that he was cool to freezing point. And it was her task to convince him that she was an efficient businesswoman capable of running a major company. She hadn't made a great start.

It was okay. It would be okay. He'd just caught her on a bad day. Tomorrow she'd be fine. She'd soon make up lost ground, demonstrate her worth. Heck, until she'd taken charge of public relations the store had been about as exciting as a dowager duchess. She'd turned it around. She could handle this.

Right now, though, she was approaching the worst moment in her life, and the last thing she needed was an encounter with Mr Frosty.

'I'm really sorry about the coffee,' she said, attempting to match him with a smile about as cool as it could get and still be a smile. 'I would have apologised if you'd given me the chance.' She waited for him to acknowledge that he should have done that. He didn't. 'Do please send me the cleaning bill for your trousers.' Not a flicker of emotion crossed his cold features and she found herself saying, 'Or you could slip out of them now and someone from Housekeeping will give them a sponge and press...'

She had been trying to help, but instead she had a mental flash of him pacing her office in boxer shorts and blushed. She never blushed. Only when she said something truly stupid. This was clearly a 'truly stupid' moment. She glanced at her watch.

'I have to be somewhere else in about ten minutes, but you're perfectly welcome to use my office while you wait,' she added, just so that he understood she wasn't going to stick around and keep him company. Trouserless.

Any other man of her acquaintance would, by now, be grinning like an idiot and praying that his luck was in. It wouldn't be, but Niall Macaulay wasn't to know that. It made no difference; he still gave her a look that would have chilled a volcano. No, she definitely couldn't compete in the coolness stakes, but at least that was a discernible reaction.

Whether it was better or worse, she couldn't say and she nervously fluffed her hair. It was a 'girly' gesture that men either loved or loathed—and one that she'd thought she'd got well under control. Clearly Mr Macaulay would loathe it. Which made it suddenly seem very attractive. She preferred any reaction, even a negative one, to nothing. So she did it again, this time loading the irritation factor by smiling at him. Not a cool smile this time, but one of those big, come-and-get-me smiles. The kind of smile that would have left the average man sitting up and begging like an eager puppy. Not Mr Macaulay. But then he wasn't average. He was more of just about anything.

He was also ice, through and through.

'Miss Claibourne, I've been asked by my cousin to spend some time shadowing you at work. Assuming, that is, you can spare valuable time from shopping to actually do any.' She followed his gaze, which had come to rest on the pile of designer bags she'd deposited on the sofa.

'Don't knock shopping, Mr Macaulay. Our ancestors invented shopping for fun. It made them rich men and it's the shopping habit that keeps the dividends rolling in.'

'Not for long, surely,' he replied, with a lift of one dark brow, 'if the directors shop elsewhere.'

She picked up her desk diary and began to flip through it—anything but meet that chilly gaze. 'You clearly have a lot to learn if you imagine couturier designers would sell anything but their *prêt-à-porter* lines through a department store. Even one as stylish as Claibourne & Faraday.' She gave a little breath of quiet satisfaction. She felt so much better for that. Then she glanced sideways at him. 'Shall we match diaries? If you can spare valuable time for such trivia?' He didn't look that excited by the prospect. His response was the merest shrug which could have meant anything, 'It's just that I can't see you and your cousins being that keen to "play shop",' she pressed.

'Play shop?' he repeated. 'I'm sorry, I didn't realise you actually served behind the counter.' It was her turn to keep silent while her brain spun wildly. India had warned her to just do her job, keep quiet and not make smart remarks. Unfortunately her mouth had a mind of its own. 'Do you?' he pressed.

'Not now,' she admitted. 'But we've all done it in the past, when we were learning the business. Do any of *you* really know the first thing about running a department store? The retail industry isn't for amateurs.'

'Really?' That at least appeared to amuse him. Or was that a suggestion that he considered her the amateur? If that were so, he did have a lot to learn.

'Really. You might be the world's greatest investment banker, but would you know how many pairs of silk knickers to order for the Christmas market?'

'Would *you*?' he asked.

Oh, yes. It had been a question in the trivia quiz on the store's website, that she'd run in the dead month of February. Before she could have the satisfaction of telling him the number, he continued, 'I'm certain you don't get that closely involved in day-to-day matters. You have department heads and buyers whose job it is to make those decisions.'

Only partly true, as she was sure he knew. 'The buck stops on the top floor, Mr Macaulay.

I'm simply making the point that I've been down there on the shop floor. I've worked in every department. I've driven delivery vans—'

'You've even been one of Santa's little helpers, according to the *Evening Post*,' he interrupted. 'How much did you learn from that?'

'Never to do it again,' she offered, with a genuine smile—one she hoped he might accept as a peace-offering. Then maybe they could stop sparring and start over. As equals.

'You didn't know about the agreement, did you?' he responded, bypassing the peace-offering and going straight for the jugular. 'That you'd have to surrender the store when your father retired?'

She was a fraction too long in telling him that he was wrong. While she was still reaching for words that wouldn't make a liar of her, he said, 'I thought not. Your father should have been honest with you all from the outset. It would have been a lot kinder.'

That would have been a first, Romana thought. If ever a man had lived with his head in the sand… 'We have no intention of meddling with the details, you know. We'll employ the best management team available to run the store—'

'*We're* the best management team available,' she retorted. Probably. She had no point of comparison. But they were family. No matter how much a high-flying executive was paid, he would never care in quite the same way. 'Leave it to us and we'll continue to deliver the profits you've enjoyed for years without ever having to lift a finger.'

'And without having any say in what happens. Profits haven't budged in three years. The store is stagnating. It's time for a change,' he announced.

Oh, knickers! The banker had done his homework. She'd bet he could tell to a penny how much they'd made in the last fiscal year. Last week, in all probability.

'The retail market has been difficult all round,' she said. She'd already said way too much. India was right. She should have kept her head down and her mouth shut.

'I know.' He sounded almost sympathetic. Romana wasn't fooled for a minute. 'But Claibourne & Farraday appears to have become entranced with its own image as the most luxurious store in London.'

'Well, it is,' she declared. 'It may not be the largest, but it has a style of its own. And it's definitely the most comfortable store in town.'

'Comfortable? As in old-fashioned, boring and lacking in new ideas?'

Romana almost winced at this telling description. 'And you have them?' she demanded. They might have sat around bemoaning their father's refusal to modernise, get away from the mahogany and red-carpet nineteenth-century decor. Let in some light. She wasn't about to tell Niall Macaulay that. 'You have brilliant new ideas?' she asked. It was far too late to keep her head down.

'Of course we have plans.' Niall Macaulay said this as if anything else was unthinkable. All buttoned-up in his dark suit, with not a scintilla of passion behind his stone-grey banker's eyes, what did he think he could bring to the greatest department store in London?

'I didn't say plans, I said *ideas*. Plans are something altogether different. You might be planning to sell out to one of the chains,' she said. 'None of the hassle, just loads of money to play with at your bank. And if you were holding the golden share, we wouldn't be able to do a thing to stop—'

'Romana...' A disembodied voice from the intercom stopped her in full flow. 'I'm sorry to interrupt, but if you don't leave right now—'

Niall Macaulay glanced at his watch. 'Five minutes to the second,' he said.

Five minutes too long, she thought. 'I'm sorry, Mr Macaulay, fascinating as this exchange of views has been, I do have to be somewhere else right now. On Claibourne & Farraday business. I'll have to leave you to compare diaries with my secretary. Just let her know when you can spare some time for the store and I'll include you in my plans.' Without waiting to listen to his views on that suggestion, she grabbed her bags and, not bothering to wait for the lift, headed for the stairs.

Spare some time? Niall wasn't about to let a chit of a girl get away with a put-down like that. She was the one not giving full value and he was about to prove it. Collecting his overcoat and umbrella, he followed her.

'Miss Claibourne?'

The uniformed commissionaire at the main entrance had summoned a taxi and was holding the door. She stepped in. She was in a hurry and didn't need another dose of Niall Macaulay. 'That didn't take long,' she said. Not nearly long enough. He'd obviously followed her straight down the stairs. Then, because politeness appeared to demand it, she said, 'Can I drop you somewhere, Mr Macaulay?'

'No.' Her relief was short-lived as he climbed in beside her. 'I'm going wherever you're going, Miss Claibourne. When I said I was going to spend some time shadowing you, I wasn't referring to some stage-managed occasion, set up for the purpose. I meant now.'

'Now?' she repeated stupidly. 'You mean now, this minute?' She laughed—an unconvincing ha-ha-ha sort of laugh—hoping that he was joking. He didn't join in. Her mistake; the man didn't joke. 'Forgive me. I understood you had a bank to run. I assumed you were a busy man, that you'd want to pick and choose.' She hoped she looked sincere when she said, 'You might prefer not to get involved in everything I do,' because she really meant it. *She* didn't want to be involved in everything she did.

'I'm here. You're here. Let's not make a performance over this. Let's just get on with it.'

He thought she was trying to hide something, and it was very tempting to say yes and let him see for himself, but really it wouldn't be a good start. 'Trust me, you really don't want to shadow me today.'

'Trust me when I say that I really do, Miss Claibourne. If I don't stay with you all the time, how will I ever learn?'

And she'd thought the taxi driver had been sarcastic.

'You don't understand. I'm not—'

'You're not working today?' He glanced at her shopping bags in a manner that suggested he wouldn't need a month to discover everything there was to know about her. His look suggested that he'd had her all weighed up from the moment half a carton of latte had taken the shine off his shoes.

'Yes, but—'

'Hadn't you better tell the driver where you want to go?'

'I really think it might be wiser if I faxed you a list of what I'll be doing for the rest of the month,' she replied firmly, ignoring his suggestion.

'I'm sure it will make interesting reading. But I particularly want to see what you're doing today.'

She doubted that. She really doubted that. A little shiver of fear erupted as a giggle. 'It's very commendable of you to take this so seriously.'

'I take everything seriously. I'm certainly not the kind of man who believes he has nothing left to learn. Even from you,' he added.

'That's very generous of you.' Her smile disguised a level of sarcasm that she rarely stooped to. Could it be catching?

'You *are* working today?' he repeated. 'You do draw a full-time salary?'

He made it sound as if she was somehow cheating. Taking the money but not putting in the work.

'Yes,' she said. 'I draw a full-time salary.' And today she was going to earn every penny, she thought, as she leaned forward to give the cab driver their destination.

India had been surprised that the Farradays had bought her delaying tactic, and it suddenly occurred to Romana that perhaps things weren't quite as simple as had first appeared. Why else would three busy men give up so much time to shadow three young women who could teach them nothing?

Niall Macaulay had already admitted that they wouldn't be running the store, but putting in their own management team. Did they need to prove the Claibourne women incompetent before they could hope to dislodge them from the boardroom?

But they weren't incompetent. So everything was just dandy...

'Miss Claibourne?'

'What? Oh... You want to see how I earn it?' she asked.

'You made a big pitch back there about how hard you all work. How nobody else could do the job.'

'I didn't say nobody. But I don't believe an investment banker could easily step into my shoes.' Not this investment banker, anyway. Public relations required warmth. An ability to smile even when you didn't feel much like it.

'Well, you've got a month to convince me. Perhaps you shouldn't waste the time.'

She glanced at him, startled by the grimness of his tone. The man certainly knew how to bear a grudge. 'You're quite sure about this? You wouldn't like to reconsider?' she asked, offering him a final chance to escape an experience she wouldn't wish on her worst enemy. She'd be happy to make an exception in his case, but she didn't want him crying foul afterwards.

'On the contrary. I'd be interested to see what you do for the fat salary you draw on top of your share of the profits. It's not a problem, is it?'

It was the word 'fat' that sealed his fate. 'Absolutely not,' she said, fastening her seatbelt. 'Be my guest.' And she dug out her cellphone and pressed a fast-dial number. 'Molly, I'm on my way. Make sure there's a spare C&F sweatshirt available.' She eyed the man next to her. 'Forty-four chest?' He made no comment on her estimate, merely regarded her suspiciously through narrowed eyes. 'That'll do. Better make it extra long. And I'll need an extra chair in my box tonight for another guest.

Niall Macaulay.' She spelt it out. 'Include him in everything this week, will you? And you'll have to double up all arrangements for the rest of the month. I'll explain when I see you.'

'Tonight?' He was regarding her through narrowed eyes. 'What's happening tonight?'

'A charity gala. Today is the start of a week of JOY, which is why your arrival is so untimely.'

'JOY?' Niall Macaulay looked slightly bemused. 'Should I know what that is?'

'A word for delight, pleasure, merriment?' she offered. 'It's also the name of the Claibourne & Farraday charity support event that we started a couple of years ago. It's a great public relations opportunity,' she added pointedly.

'Oh, yes. I remember reading about it in the annual report.'

What else? 'We do it every year and raise a lot of cash for under-privileged children.'

'And get a lot of free publicity at the same time.'

At last! 'It's not exactly free. You wouldn't believe the cost of balloons these days. And sweatshirts. But it's good value for money, especially for the children. Of course we do have a very good public relations department.' She smiled at him, but only because that seemed to annoy him most. 'You didn't think this was a nine-to-five job, did you? I don't keep bank hours, I'm afraid.' Then, 'I'm sorry, will your wife be expecting you home?' She was catching onto this sarcastic lark. She was rather afraid she might get to enjoy it.

'I'm not married, Miss Claibourne,' he replied. 'I haven't been for some time.'

Romana wasn't in the least bit surprised.

CHAPTER TWO

NIALL took out his mobile phone and called his secretary, reorganising his schedule for the rest of the day, dealing with queries that wouldn't wait. At least the evening presented no problems. His date with a report on the steel industry would keep.

Romana was making calls too. One after another. Talking to an endless stream of people involved in the gala, checking last-minute details about flowers and programmes and seating.

It was possible she was attempting to impress him. Or maybe she was simply avoiding conversation. For that, at least, he should be grateful.

Staring out at the passing streets as the driver edged slowly through the city in the heavy midday traffic, he had plenty of time to regret the impulse that had prompted him to follow Romana Claibourne out of the office.

Heaven alone knew that he didn't want to spend a minute in her company that wasn't absolutely necessary. He had precious little time for ditzy blondes at the best of times. He had none at all for those who played at being 'company director' in the little time they could spare from shopping. He glanced at the designer label carrier bags, scattered about her long, narrow feet.

Encased in designer shoes with a price ticket to reflect the label, he had no doubt.

His lip curled at such conspicuous extravagance even while the man in him recognised the beauty of the feet, the slender ankles and the legs to which they were attached. There was a lot of leg to admire—Romana Claibourne clearly didn't believe in hiding her best features.

She was pushing back her wild, thick mane of curls when she realised that he was staring at her. Every instinct warned him to turn away as she paused, querying his look. Instead, he did what he knew would most irritate her. He raised one brow...bored, unimpressed...and turned back to the more interesting view of passing traffic.

A charity gala, no matter how good the cause, wasn't his idea of work. It wasn't even his idea of fun. Such events were right at the bottom of his 'must-do' list. He'd far rather send a cheque and pass on the manufactured glamour.

But he could scarcely complain. She'd given him every opportunity to escape, offered to sort out the shadowing in a civilised manner; he'd simply assumed she was trying to get rid of him in order to get on with whatever that overnight bag had been packed for.

It was too late now to wish he'd simply asked her what she was doing for the rest of day. There was just something about the girl, the way she looked at him with those big blue eyes as if she was used to twisting men around her little finger and having them sit up and beg for more. He'd wanted her to know that he was made of sterner stuff.

The taxi finally came to a halt just upstream of Tower Bridge, where the burgundy and gold livery of Claibourne & Farraday was much in evidence on balloons and sweatshirts and a huge crowd was being whipped up into a state of wild excitement for the television cameras.

'We're here, Mr Macaulay.'

'Niall, please,' he said. Not out of any desire for informality, but because a whole month of being addressed as ''Mr Macaulay'' in a manner just short of insolent was not going to improve his temper.

And he could see for himself that they'd arrived.

It was what they were going to be doing that bothered him. Then, as he stepped out of the taxi and saw the C&F banner draped over the length of a very tall crane and a huge sign inviting participants to 'Jump for JOY', it became blindingly obvious.

He discovered that charity galas were not, after all, at the bottom of his list.

Charity bungee-jumping was right off the page.

'It's not always like this,' Romana said, as she turned from paying the cab driver. 'Some days are quite dull.' She tucked the receipt into her wallet, then looked up and flashed a quick smile at him. 'Although not many—not if I can help it.'

'You're going to jump?' he asked. Silly question. Of course she was going to jump. She was being paid to have fun and she was enjoying every stupid, reckless minute of it.

'Do you wish you'd gone back to your office when you had a chance, shadow-man?' The challenge was light enough, but it was unmistakable. It said, *Where I go, you follow.*

'Not at all,' he replied. 'I'm finding the experience highly informative, but you appear to have misinterpreted the word ''shadow''. You could have saved yourself the bother of organising a sweatshirt for me. I'm not playing follow-my-leader, Romana. I'm simply observing.'

She glanced up at him. 'Scared, huh?'

He let that go. He had nothing to prove. There had been a time when he'd been as reckless as a man could be. But life had a way of mocking you. The gentlest of pastimes could be more dangerous than jumping into thin air.

'Have you ever done this before?' he asked.

'Me? Good grief, no. I'm scared of heights.' For a moment he believed her, then, when she had him hooked, she grinned. 'How else do you think I managed to drum up so much sponsorship?'

'You could have pinned your victims down and threatened to pour coffee over them unless they signed on the dotted line?' he offered. She was bright and bubbly, and no doubt very good at this kind of mindless nonsense, but she wasn't his idea of a company director.

She acknowledged his bull's-eye with the slightest nod. 'I'll bear that in mind for next year. Thanks for the tip.'

'There won't be a next year.'

'Well, no, not a bungee-jump, but...' She suddenly realised that he wasn't referring to the bungee-jump, but the imminent eviction of the Claibournes from the boardroom. 'But I'll come up with something equally exciting,' she continued firmly. 'If you'd like to show your own enthusiasm it's not too late to phone your office and drum up some sponsorship yourself. It's for a great cause, and I'm sure there are any number of people who'd pay good money to see you jump a hundred feet from a crane with an elastic band tied to your feet.' Her smile was gratingly sweet as she offered him her phone. 'It's being broadcast on the internet,' she added, 'so they'll be able to watch the whole thing live and get their money's worth.' Then, because she couldn't resist it, 'I'll sponsor you myself.'

He'd just bet she would, but he shook his head. 'I'll stick to the arrangement we made. You do whatever you usually do. I'll observe.' No hardship on the eye, at least. Just on the brain. 'You *are* jumping?'

'One of the Claibournes had to make the opening jump and since India and Flora suddenly discovered pressing appointments elsewhere…' She shrugged. 'It's a pity, though. If I'd known you'd be here I could have billed us both as the opening jump. We've already got the front page of *Celebrity* magazine for next week, but with you arriving out of the blue we could have sold pictures to the financial pages, too.'

'How much have you raised in sponsorship?'

'Personally?' She glanced up at the crane. 'Is it worth risking my neck for fifty-three thousand pounds do you think?'

'Fifty-three thousand pounds?' He was impressed, but he wasn't about to show it. 'That many people want to see you scared to death?'

'Scared to death?' Her eyes widened, making them appear impossibly large.

'Isn't that the point? You make a big thing out of being terrified of heights so your sponsors pay out to hear you scream.'

There was a pause before she said, 'I must make sure to give them value for money. Thanks for reminding me,' she said as her attention was claimed by a young woman bearing a sweatshirt.

'Who's the dishy bloke?'

'Dishy?' Romana didn't have to follow her

assistant's avid gaze. Molly could only be talking about Niall. 'He's not dishy.' He was mind-numbingly gorgeous. The kind of man that would have a girl dropping coffee and everything else if he so much as smiled. Maybe that was why he didn't smile. It was too dangerous.

'Crumbs, Romana, get your eyes tested. You don't often get tall, dark and the look of the devil all in one package.'

That summed him up perfectly, and she felt a little tremor somewhere in her midriff that had nothing at all to do with jumping into space. 'Should a married woman be having such thoughts about a man who is not her husband?'

'I'm married, Romana. Not dead.'

'Well, you can put your eyes back in their sockets. He might be good to look at but I promise you he's not nice to know. The man is dour. With a capital D. A real cold fish. His name is Niall Macaulay and he's one of the Farraday clan—'

'I didn't know there were any real live Farradays.'

'Unfortunately they're as real and as live as you can get. This one is a dominant male of the species and he's going to be shadowing my role with the company for the next month.' And marking her out of ten for technique. She didn't think he'd be interested in artistic merit.

'You mean he's the one being squeezed into your box at the gala tonight? You lucky cow! Do you think he'd like some coffee?' she asked hopefully.

'He needs something,' she said, with feeling. 'A charm implant would be a definite improvement. But I'd advise against offering him coffee if you value your life.' She looked up at the crane and shivered. 'One of us has to be at the gala this evening.'

'You'll be fine. Just don't forget to smile for the cameras. It'll probably be the cover picture, so when you put on that sweatshirt make sure the C&F logo is front and centre. I'd stay and help, but I have to meet the caterers at the theatre.'

Smile for the camera? *Smile?*

A teeth-baring grimace was all she could manage as she stared in the mirror and re-touched her lipstick for the television camera which would follow her every move once she emerged from the caravan. She'd have bitten it all off long before she reached the jump plat-form. Not good. She put the lipstick in her pocket, along with her handbag mirror, for a last-minute touch-up. If she could keep her hand sufficiently steady.

She caught herself fluffing her hair. Again. Holding her arms firmly at her sides, she fixed a smile to her lips and emerged from the car-avan to be met by the television director.

'Great,' she said absently as he ran through what would happen. But her mind was some-where else. On Niall Macaulay, who was standing a few yards away. It was hard to tell if he was regretting his decision to join her. His expression gave nothing away. 'Sure you won't join me, Niall? A Farraday jumping would be the icing on the cake. And it would really prove your commitment.'

The director spun to look at him. 'Hey, this is great. If you could just change as quickly as you can, Mr Farraday—'

'The name is Macaulay.' The director looked confused. 'Niall Farraday Macaulay. And there are more than enough people around here desperate to fling themselves into space for a good cause. I don't want to be selfish and hold things up.' Romana gave him a look that suggested he wasn't fooling her with his lack of selfishness. 'I'll sponsor Miss Claibourne instead.'

Romana was temporarily speechless. It was the second time he'd done that to her today, and she didn't like it.

'Niall Farraday Macaulay?' she asked him as she went to weigh in. 'You really are called that?'

'It's a family tradition. A reminder that our time will come.'

'Not if I can help it,' she said. Then turned away to take the card to be handed to the jump team. She took it in fingers that were losing any sense of feeling. Only her mouth was working, running away with her, joking to the camera about getting vertigo standing on a high kerb...

It avoided having to think about what was ahead.

She wasn't thinking at all, or she might have distracted the photographer from *Celebrity* magazine when he wanted to take a picture of the two of them together. Yet, even numb with terror, the PR side of her brain was saying *Go for it!* This would get people talking, create a buzz...and wasn't it vital to demonstrate her ability to take advantage of a photo opportunity?

'Claibourne & Farraday working in partnership for deprived children everywhere,' she prompted, offering a hand to Niall. Her jumping and him watching. Nothing new there.

He sketched a smile, as if he knew exactly what she was thinking. He probably did, she realised, and felt instantly guilty; there might be some perfectly good reason for his lack of good humour. And for not taking part in the jump.

A solid grasp of the principles of gravity and plain good sense, perhaps?

'Get really close, warm and caring...' the photographer encouraged. Niall was surprisingly co-operative, putting his arm around her shoulders before she could reconsider. It felt almost shockingly good to be tucked up against him. 'Lovely...big smile...'

Startled by the direction her thoughts were taking, she glanced up at him. The breeze from the river was whipping up his perfectly cut hair and feathering it across his forehead, and as he smiled to order it was plain that, physically, the man had everything. Style, good looks and a set of teeth any film star would pay a fortune for.

The minute the photographer finished, Niall let his arm drop. The smile, however, remained. A warning that she had indeed made a mistake by drawing attention to his presence. It was something the columnist at *Celebrity* would seize on and speculate about at length. And if his photograph appeared on the front cover India would never forgive her.

'They're waiting for you,' he said, the smile turning into the smallest of frowns as she stepped onto the hoist with legs that didn't appear to belong to her and made a grab for the safety rail as it began to rise. Had he realised how scared she was? Did it matter?

'What's the view like?' The presenter's voice in her ear prompted her.

Aware that the mini-cam would be picking up the fact that her eyes were tight shut, she managed to blurt out, 'I'm saving it for a surprise when I get to the top.'

The sound of laughter reached her over the loudspeaker, and as the hoist came to a halt she instinctively opened her eyes as she stepped onto the platform. Big mistake. Behind her, her escape route returned to the ground. In front of her London seemed to shift beneath her feet and she felt the colour drain from her face.

'I'd like to go home now,' she said, grabbing the first solid object that came to hand. Everyone laughed.

She joined in, trying not to sound hysterical. But she was out of time. As the hoist came to a halt behind her, with its first load of paying jumpers, she said, 'Could someone unpeel my fingers from this rail?'

'I thought this was all in a day's work for you.'

Niall Macaulay. Riding to her rescue. She knew he'd seen her fear… 'You dropped this.' He handed her the card with her name and weight on it. 'I wouldn't want you to miss out on the excitement.'

She glanced at the card, frowning at the implication that she had tried to get out of jumping. She would have turned and glared at him for being such a know-all, but she wasn't prepared to move that much. Besides, this was a live broadcast.

'Well, thanks. It's good to see Claibourne & Farraday working together.' Even *in extremis* she still remembered to mention the company name.

'No problem. It's what a shadow's for. To pick up the mistakes. Can I offer some help there?'

More sarcasm, but Romana was beyond caring about the feud. Her knuckles were bonewhite as she gripped the cold metal.

'My hero,' she said, as Niall peeled her fingers one by one from the rail.

The bungee-team, eager to get started, fixed up the bungee. When they'd finished, it was Niall who reached out a hand to help her to her feet. It was oddly comforting, and she kept her eyes fixed on his face. That way she wasn't so conscious of the drop. There were creases at the corners of his eyes, she noticed, as if smiling hadn't always been such a strain. 'It's quite normal to be scared,' he said.

'Scared? Who's scared?' She put the fingers of her other hand in her mouth and pulled a face at the camera. Clowning was the only way she was going to get through this.

'It's safer than falling out of bed,' he assured her.

'You can guarantee that?' she asked. 'You've tested the theory? How many beds have you fallen out of?' The grammar wasn't great, but it raised a laugh from the crowd and stopped Niall Macaulay from smiling. A hundred-percent success.

'Ready, Romana?'

Belatedly recalling Molly's reminder to smile, she retrieved her hand from Niall, took out her mirror and lipstick and made a big performance of retouching the colour. 'Got to look good in the photographs,' she said, beyond shaking. She wasn't feeling anything very much at all, just a sort of numb weightlessness, and she bared her teeth in the nearest approximation to a smile she could manage. '*Now* I'm ready.' She handed the lipstick and mirror to Niall. 'Any last-minute advice?'

'Don't look down?' He picked her up from behind and for a moment held her hard against his chest. The warmth was welcome, and for the first time since she'd stepped onto the hoist she felt safe. Then he took a step forward.

A gasp of fright escaped her. 'Are you going to throw me over?' She'd intended to whisper, but the microphone attached to her sweatshirt picked up every syllable.

'Not this time,' he murmured, his response covered by a burst of laughter. Then he placed her carefully on the edge of the platform, with her toes sticking out into clear space. Her toes didn't like it, and clawed desperately at the inside of her shoes. Only his hand, still on her shoulder, was keeping her from fainting. Actually, that wasn't such a bad idea...

'On the count of three,' he murmured against her ear. 'And don't forget to scream.'

CHAPTER THREE

NIALL watched Romana fly. It was a spectacular jump by any standards. Only an underlying suspicion that she was actually scared rigid had prompted him to bring up the card.

Watching her in the hoist, he'd been sure that she was going to lose it completely. And, no matter who was running the company, he had a financial stake in its image.

He should have known that the fooling around was for the camera. He hadn't been sure until she'd pulled out the lipstick, but her hands had been steady as a rock. It was all just part of the act. She'd certainly put on a show for her sponsors.

All she'd forgotten was the blood-curdling scream.

Someone opened a bottle of champagne and pushed a glass into her hand. Romana didn't dare put it to her mouth. The glass would have shattered against her chattering teeth. She just gripped it tightly as around her the crowd chanted a slow countdown for the next jumper.

For a moment she thought she'd be all right, but just as the next bungee reached its full length and then snapped back her entire stomach relived her own experience. She pushed the glass into the hand of the person standing nearest to her and fled to the caravan so that she could be violently sick in private.

When she'd washed her face, and rinsed her mouth out with water, she realised that her phone, still lying on the chair where she had abandoned it earlier, was ringing.

'Ramona Claibourne.'

It was Molly. 'Are you all right? We've got a television on here, and when I saw you make a run for it I wondered—'

'If breakfast was a mistake? Believe me, it was. Is everyone demanding their money back?' She was still shaking. 'I wouldn't blame them. I couldn't even manage a decent scream. My throat was apparently stuffed with hot rocks.'

'Don't worry about it. You looked terrific. And the jokey stuff was very convincing. I shouldn't think anyone guessed how scared you really were. I can't imagine how you'll top it next year—unless you can think of something that involves Mr Dour getting his shirt off,' she added hopefully. 'I'd sponsor him for that myself.'

Ramona's mouth dried at the thought. Fortunately there was a sharp rap at the door and she was saved from having to comment.

'It's open,' she called, and turned to see the man himself, with a frown that might have been concern creasing his forehead. She didn't want his concern. 'Come to pay up?' she asked, with a lack of graciousness she regretted the minute he laid a cheque on the table, along with her lipstick and mirror. 'That's very generous,' she said. 'Thank you.'

He gave a small shrug, as if it was nothing. 'Don't let me interrupt your call.'

'Oh, it's just Molly. She saw the jump...' The least said about that the better. 'She's trying to think of some way of topping it. She seems to think you, minus your shirt, would be a good start,' she said, and was assailed by wails of anguish from her assistant. 'Why don't you talk it over with her?' she suggested, handing over her phone. 'And she'll need your address so that she can book you a car for tonight. Six o'clock. Black tie.'

'Six?' he repeated. 'Isn't that a little early for the theatre?'

'I'm working, not having fun. I do all the organising beforehand. I make sure everything goes smoothly throughout the evening, and then I make sure everyone is happy afterwards.'

'While I watch?'

'No one is insisting you come, Niall. You're the one demanding to see what I do every minute of my working day.' Which today would end somewhere past midnight.

She turned away, avoiding a game of 'chicken' to see who could outstare the other.

She knew she'd lose. She didn't bother to change back into her suit, but folded it neatly and put it into her bag, then glanced in the mirror as she slid her fingers through her hair in an attempt to tame it.

Her reflection warned her that she was looking less than her best. The colour had leached from her skin, leaving two vivid patches of blusher and making her look like a rag doll. She took a tissue and scrubbed at her cheekbones. In the meantime, having considered her response and apparently got the message, Niall relayed his address to Molly.

Romana retrieved her phone and her bags and flung open the caravan door.

'Where are you going now?' he asked, following her.

'Why don't you come along and see?' He gave her a look that suggested he was quick learner—he was asking first. 'First I'm going home to hang up my dress. I would have done it earlier, but I had to meet you instead. Then I'm going back to the store to have my hair done,' she told him, walking quickly to the road.

'No lunch?'

She felt ill at the thought. 'No,' she said, glancing at the workmanlike watch on her wrist. 'No time. We have to go.'

'Thanks, but I think I'll pass on the hairdo.'

'Good decision. I can fix most things,' she said, and smiled, 'but an appointment with George on a gala night is not one of them. I'll see you at the theatre.'

'Don't you think it would be more sensible for us to share a car?'

Share? Working with him was going to be difficult enough; she had no intention of extending the time they spent together. 'Is your concern ecological or financial?'

'Neither. I simply thought you could brief me about this evening on the way to the theatre. Speaking of which, you put on quite a performance yourself just now,' he said, keeping step with her and giving her no chance to argue. 'You nearly had me fooled.'

She had no way of telling whether he meant her performance pretending to be scared, or her performance covering up the fact that she was totally terrified. 'Only nearly?'

'How many jumps have you made?'

She smiled as she stopped and turned to hail a passing taxi. There was something very pleasing in the discovery that he wasn't nearly as clever as he thought he was.

'I'll see you at the theatre, Niall,' she said as she climbed aboard, shutting the door firmly behind her.

Romana, swathed in a dark-red salon wrapper, regarded herself in the mirror, searching vainly for some clue as to what about her appearance had so irritated Niall Macaulay.

It couldn't just have been the incident with the coffee that had made him so surly. It had, after all, been an accident. Unfortunate, perhaps, especially in view of the subsequent meeting, but in the travails of life it was nothing. Less than nothing.

A kind man would have said so. A generous man would at the very least have allowed her to apologise before walking away.

But he wasn't kind, or generous. Oh, he'd been quick to cover himself with his offer of sponsorship—quick to pay up, too. Her flash of guilt was immediately squashed. When you had money to spare, that kind of generosity was easy. Her father had always been swift to put his signature on a cheque for birthdays or at Christmas, when all she'd really wanted was for him to hug her, tell her that he loved her. He'd never seemed capable of managing anything quite that difficult.

George appeared in the mirror behind her. 'Big day, Romana,' he said.

'A bad day.' First bungee-jumping. Then a haircut. How much worse could one day get?

'No sacrifice is too great to promote the store.'

'This is as far as I'm prepared to go,' she assured him. The haircut was all part of the week of publicity for the store and had been planned for months. Faced with proving her total commitment, she knew nothing would make a more public statement than cutting her trademark hair to publicise the salon.

The stylist hesitated, apparently not eager to be the cause of bitter tears of regret. 'You're really sure about this? I should warn you that while your girlfriends will love it—'

'Great. They're the ones to impress. Let's do it.' Still he hesitated. 'Come on, George, I haven't got all day.'

'You do realise that the men in your life will hate it?'

'Who has the time for men?'

'Friends, acquaintances, your father?'

'I stopped being Daddy's little girl when I was four.' When her mother had found some-one younger, better-looking, even titled...

'Any man you've ever met, then. Any man who's ever seen your photograph in the gossip mags. You must be aware that half the men in London are in love with your hair. They'll want to lynch me—'

'What's a little pain if it means you'll get your picture in the papers?' Still he hesitated.

'I know. I'll get used to it. Probably. Any last-minute panics? How's it going at the theatre?'

'Relax. The programmes have been delivered, the florists are arranging for England and the caterers are all set. No one has cancelled. Everything is running like silk.'

'Those are words calculated to freeze the blood in my veins.'

'You worry too much.'

'That's an impossibility.'

'Honestly, everything's organised to the last ...top.' Then, 'I saw your hunk, by the way. ...Buttery when I picked up your sand-

...ana frowned. 'My hunk? Since when ...ve a hunk to call my own?'

'...not so much a hunk,' Molly replied ...gly. 'He's more your James Bond ..., dark and deadly. If he were shad-...he wouldn't be eating alone.'

Then, belatedly catching on, 'Are ...me that Niall Macaulay is in the

'For heaven's sake, George, it's just hair. Cut it.'

And for the second time that day she closed her eyes.

Niall Macaulay looked up at the impressive façade of Claibourne & Farraday. Once a small emporium catering exclusively to the aristocracy, it had, over the generations, expanded until it occupied one of the most valuable pieces of real estate in London.

Jordan was obsessed with the need to reclaim it for the sake of family pride. Bram's mind took a more logical path—the Farraday claim had to be protected in the face of a raft of new legislation.

A new agreement, something more equitable, would certainly put an end to the feud mentality that had prevailed among the older generation since control of the store had shifted from the Farradays to the Claibournes. It had been at a time when the women's movement had been gaining ground, and Jordan's mother had expected her claim to be taken seriously. Jordan had never forgiven Peter Claibourne for brushing her aside, and Jordan had been brought up listening to her complaining about it.

Niall's own desire to claim the 'golden share' had nothing to do with sentiment. Romana Claibourne was right. He wanted control so that they would be in a position to liquidise the assets and reinvest the money in something less subject to the whim of public taste. The retail sector was a minefield, definitely not a place for the unwary.

With a nod to the doorman who opened one of the huge doors for him, he paused on the threshold to gain his bearings. While one of C&F's burgundy and gold liveried vans delivered his weekly groceries, it had been more than four years since he'd actually walked around the store.

He'd been with Louise. Choosing china, bedlinen, touring the departments, making a wedding list. He'd left all the decisions to her... It was to be her house; he'd wanted her to have everything just as she wanted it. All

he'd wanted to do was watch her. Be with her. See her lovely face change from query as she turned to ask his opinion, knowing his answ would be the same— ''You choose'' —to a smile...

He ached at the memory, but that hap was long gone. And this would be his portunity to reacquaint himself store—check out any changes—as just one more browsing custome morrow everyone would know

He'd better make the most he'd missed lunch, he'd begin the restaurants.

Romana reached up on au when her hand encounte where her hair had on

'Eat this and stop hair looks wonderf sandwich she'd br hoping to tempt a genius.'

'Well, yes. I assumed you'd come back to-gether. You didn't know he was here?'

'No, I did not. Of all the sneaky... Did he see you?'

'I don't think so. He was talking to someone on his mobile, and after your toe-curling sug-gestion that I was smitten with him there was no way I was going across to ask if he was enjoying his lunch. He might he gorgeous to look at, but you're right—he is a bit daunting. Not the kind of man you'd wave at in a res-taurant on such short acquaintance.'

'I wouldn't wave at him if I were drowning. Call Security, please, Molly.'

She looked aghast. 'You're not going to have him thrown out!'

'Of course not. I simply want to know what he's up to.'

Common sense told her that he could have been in the store every day for the last year, compiling a whole host of black marks against the Claibourne clan. Intuition warned her that this wasn't so, that he was merely taking his last chance of anonymity to look around on his own. It was, after all, exactly what she'd have done in his shoes. But she wasn't leaving anything to chance.

'I want to know everywhere he goes, who he talks to, what he looks at. Any incidents. I want a full report on my desk first thing in the morning.'

Niall checked out all the restaurants and coffee shops, each very different. There was even a Japanese-style sushi bar, which surprised him. All of them were busy.

He ate his belated lunch in the Buttery, only because it looked the least inspired of the choices available. He gave it perhaps six out of ten. And he was being generous.

Leaving the restaurant, he began to tour the store. It hadn't changed noticeably since the refit in the early twentieth century, and was still steeped in the dated luxury of mahogany and burgundy carpeting that was the store's signature.

The customer base was younger than he'd anticipated, though.

The Claibournes must be doing something right.

Jordan wouldn't want to hear that. He only wanted to know what they were doing wrong.

He first noticed that he had a 'tail' as he wandered through the book department.

It was, he thought, a poor use of expensive selling space. Typical of a department that had once been popular but had outlived its time. It couldn't compete with the new bookstore chains, with their coffee shops and cut prices.

He took her by surprise as he stopped to make a note and the woman following him turned away a little too quickly, drawing attention to herself.

He'd seen Romana's assistant dash into the Buttery. She hadn't acknowledged his presence and he'd assumed she hadn't seen him. It would appear that he was making rather too many assumptions.

In his wide experience of human nature he'd learned to trust first impressions, that glimpse of the unguarded personality before a man or woman realised they were being observed.

Romana Claibourne had climbed out of a taxi hampered by a clutch of carrier bags, in heels a touch too high for good sense and a skirt too short for anyone who anticipated being taken seriously. And with enough hair to stuff a mattress flying in all directions. His first impression had been of a scatty mantrap who wouldn't hesitate to use her looks to get what she wanted.

He didn't doubt for a moment that she usually got it.

Scatty or not, she'd wasted no time in sending a store detective to keep an eye on him, check what he was up to. That took some nerve, he thought as he glanced at his watch and headed for the exit, determined to fit in a couple of hours at his own desk before the gala.

But he really couldn't let her get away with the idea she'd outsmarted him.

Romana was on the point of leaving when Molly caught up with her at the lift.

'I can't stop—'

'You'll want to know about this.' She handed her a shiny burgundy gift-carrier, with Claibourne & Farraday in copperplate gold lettering.

'What is this?'

'The store detective you sent to shadow your shadow just brought this up to the office. Mr Macaulay asked her to give it to you with his compliments.'

She groaned. 'He spotted her?'

'Apparently.' The girl was grinning.

'It's not funny, Molly.'

Her giggle suggested otherwise. Romana opened the bag. Nestling inside was a carton of a new scent that had been on display that week. *Summer Shadow.*

'I do love a man with a sense of humour, don't you?'

'This isn't humour,' Romana snapped. 'The man hasn't got a sense of humour. This is...' She hesitated. She'd been going to say sarcasm. Again. But it was subtler than that. '...irony.'

*   *   *

Niall fastened the studs in his shirt, then picked up his bow-tie. Louise had joked that he'd only married her because he couldn't tie the thing himself.

Four years. She'd been gone four years. Four years of a life so empty that it echoed like an unfurnished room.

He picked up the photograph in the heavy silver frame that stood on the dressing table, lightly touched the lovely face that smiled back at him. Dark, aristocratic—the complete opposite of Romana Claibourne in every way, he told himself.

Then, quite unexpectedly, he found Romana's riveting blue eyes intruding between them. And for a split second he couldn't tell the difference.

Romana fastened the platinum wire choker about her throat and the matching cuffs on her wrists—they were part of the African collection commissioned by Flora after her research trip the previous year, and they'd just gone on sale in the store. The simplicity would offer a stark contrast to the diamonds that Her Royal Highness would be wearing to the gala; there was absolutely no point in trying to compete.

She'd kept her dress simple too. Understated. Tonight she was one of the supporting cast, ensuring that things ran smoothly behind the scenes while India took centre stage. But she still had to look perfect. Hair, nails, make-up. Everything but the dress a showcase for the store.

Was Niall right about that? Should she be wearing something from their own fashion department? But then it was so much easier for men. A well-cut dinner jacket and a starched shirt was all it took. They could wear the same suit, shirt, cuff-links for years and no one would notice. But still...

She'd worked so hard on building a fresh, lively new image for the store. Still had so much to do. For the first time she seriously began to consider the possibility of losing it. And how much that would hurt. She could not let that happen.

She picked up the scent Niall had sent her and wondered if she'd underestimated the man. Not intellectually. She didn't doubt for a moment that he was clever with a capital C. But was it possible that, in spite of all evidence to the contrary, he understood the retail sector?

That he had a sense of humour?

On an impulse, she sprayed her wrists with the fragrance. It was green and cool, like the beautiful opaque glass container. Cool as Niall Macaulay. She found herself smiling. Whatever else he was, when it came to making a point, the man wasn't cheap.

And not always cold, she thought, remembering how warm and safe she'd felt with his arm about her. How, just for a moment, she'd forgotten that she was scared to death.

A ring on the doorbell brought her back to reality and she dropped the scent as if burned, scarcely believing that she'd used it.

The reality was that Niall Macaulay was the enemy, plotting to claim Claibourne & Farraday for his own. As she picked up her wrap and her bag and headed for the door, she said out loud, 'It isn't going to happen.'

She wasn't going to let it happen.

CHAPTER FOUR

NIALL crossed the cordoned-off section of pavement where the television camera was already set up and the paparazzi were already camped out. No one took any notice of him. He was too early to be anyone interesting.

He showed the pass Molly had entrusted to the driver of the car sent to collect him and was admitted to the theatre. Every pillar in the foyer was entwined from floor to ceiling with flowers and tiny white lights, a triumph of the florist's art. And centre stage, exactly where he'd expected her to be, was Romana Claibourne, directing the positioning of a display board.

She was wearing a simple, unadorned figure-hugging dress of dark blue satin, a miracle of tailoring that clung to her curves without any visible means of support. It didn't need adornment. Stunning in its simplicity, its style, it was the kind of dress designed to make a man long to get his hands on it—and the figure it so inadequately concealed.

A man who'd lived in a sexual limbo, unresponsive to even the most seductive advances since the death of the woman he'd loved, he found his unexpectedly earthy response to Romana Claibourne's volatile charms deeply shocking.

And it wasn't just the figure-hugging dress but her hair that claimed his attention. The wild—and, to him, unappealing—mane had gone, and now a tumble of tiny curls framed her face, curling onto the nape of her long and very beautiful neck. She'd highlighted its exposure with a choker made from dozens of thin strands of platinum wire. It gave her the appearance of some African queen.

She had been transformed from a ditzy-looking blonde he'd have crossed the road to avoid into the most stunning young woman. A man, if he didn't have a care, could lose his head. And his heart.

He took an instinctive step backward, as if the thought threatened him in some way. How could it? He didn't have a heart to lose. He'd given it without reservation to the only woman he would ever love.

But the men struggling to place the heavy boards exactly where she wanted them appeared to have lost theirs to Romana, falling over themselves to please her as she flattered and flirted with them.

He stayed where he was for a while, watching as she had them move the display four times before she was entirely happy with the result. Throughout the operation she was courteous, charming, and when they had done exactly as she wanted her smile was angelic. They were her slaves.

Once again he was torn between the cynical belief that she was simply using her very obvious feminine appeal to get what she wanted and a disconcerting certainty that her charm was the real thing.

Putting his trust in cynicism, he crossed the thick carpet to join her before she turned and caught him standing in the shadows.

'Good evening, Romana,' he said, glancing at the boards, curious to see what all the fuss had been about.

Romana half turned. 'Oh, Niall, you've arrived,' she said, and he could tell, from the slight edge to her voice, the slight flush to her cheeks, that she'd been aware of him the moment he'd arrived. His skin prickled with tension, every cell in his body suddenly on fire; the fact that they were adversaries only served to heighten his awareness of her. 'Just when the hard work has been done.'

The sharpness betrayed her. The attraction was mutual. He felt a quick surge of power. The forgotten thrill of mentally fencing with a beautiful woman, knowing it could only end in one place. The fact that it was impossible lent an extra edge of danger.

'On the contrary, I watched proceedings with every bit as much interest as you.' He raised a brow, daring her to suggest she'd done anything more than direct operations. 'That is what I'm supposed to be doing, isn't it? Watching? If you'd wanted another porter—'

She held up a hand, stopping him with an elegant gesture. She wore bracelets—cuffs of platinum wire that matched the choker at her throat—on each wrist. As she raised her hand the strands of platinum rippled against smooth ivory skin. 'You've made your point, Niall. You're here to observe, not take part.' For a moment she looked at him as if she could see right through him, read his mind. But then, how hard could it be? She indicated the display board. 'So. Observe.'

He found it harder than it should have been to turn away and look at the photographic collage of the projects supported by the charity week, the happy children it had helped. A perfect example of a picture being worth a thousand words. 'Very impressive.' He watched her reach up to adjust a photograph that had become loose during the move. 'And it's very effective PR.'

'How cynical you are, Niall.'

'Am I wrong?' he asked.

She looked as if she might tell him just how wrong he was. What she said was, 'No, of course not.'

He'd rather have heard what she was really thinking. 'What do you do for the rest of the year?' he asked. 'I imagine one bungee-jump goes a long way.'

'It seemed like for ever,' she replied, and glanced back at him briefly.

He saw again an echo of fear in her eyes. It was gone in a heartbeat, but she wouldn't fool him again.

'You're right, though,' she added. 'It isn't all champagne and glamour.'

She finished smoothing the photograph and stepped back to admire the finished effect while she recovered herself. It took no time at all, apparently, because she turned and looked up at him with a smile that suggested she was quite over her fright. A tiny, mischievous smile. 'I'm so sorry, Niall. I forgot to thank you for the scent. I'm—'

'I'm glad you received it safely,' he said, quickly cutting her off before she said something totally outrageous. Or repeated her accusation of cynicism.

'I'm wearing it tonight,' she finished, refusing to be thwarted. And she lifted her hand, the strands of platinum shimmering enticingly as they slipped back, to offer him her slender wrist.

He'd bought the scent solely for its name. Confronted with the reality, he found himself longing to take her wrist, lift it to his face, touch it to his lips. To hold her and tell her she must never, never do anything that scared her ever again.

Which was doubtless just what she meant him to feel. She really was the most accomplished flirt. Was it a conscious decision to distract him? Or did it just come naturally to her?

Whatever, he really couldn't allow her to think he was that gullible. 'As a penance?' he enquired, ignoring her proffered wrist. 'It really wasn't necessary. In fact the assistant insisted on telling me that it was for daytime wear. Was she wrong? Or merely incompetent?'

If he'd hoped to irritate her by criticising the store personnel, leaving her with her wrist extended and no one to fawn over it, he'd failed miserably. She frowned, but not with annoyance.

'May I?' she said, and without waiting for an answer she reached for his tie, straightening it, twitching it into place with the lightest of tugs, the gentlest of touches.

It was the most intimate of gestures, evoking bittersweet memories of Louise and a sharp guilt that moments before he'd had nothing, no one, in his head but Romana Claibourne. But before he could react, move, it was over.

'That's better,' she said, leaning back a little. 'Even shadows have to be perfect in every detail.' Then, apparently satisfied, she looked up and answered his question. 'I'm sure the assistant knew exactly what she was talking about, Niall. I don't normally wear scent to the theatre...there's nothing worse than sitting near someone wearing an overpowering perfume, is there? This is light, though.' And she lifted the inside of her wrist to sample it for herself. 'Quite...inoffensive.' But she didn't offer her wrist a second time for his opinion.

It had occurred to him, belatedly, that scent was such a personal gift that she might have been insulted by his gesture. He'd certainly never expected her to wear it. Now, dragging his thoughts back to the present, to reality, he said, 'It was not my intention to offend you.'

'Then well done,' she said, gravely. 'You succeeded.' Only a tiny tuck in the corner of her mouth betrayed her.

The wretched girl had been teasing him. Still was.

'Romana...' She turned away as her sister arrived, saving him from the need to respond. Giving him time to catch his breath. 'Everything looks wonderful.'

'Yes, Molly's done a fine job. India, may I introduce Niall Farraday Macaulay? He's begun the arduous task of shadowing me, as you can see.'

India Claibourne, taller than her sister, with her dark hair perfectly cut in a sleek bob, was quite unlike Romana. Turning to him now with a cool smile, she offered her hand briefly. 'You're very keen, Mr Macaulay.' Despite the polite smile she was unable to disguise the edge in her voice.

'I wouldn't have put it quite like that, Miss Claibourne. Romana explained that her job isn't confined to the hours between nine and five. I'm making every effort to be fair.'

'None of us work nine to five—as you and your partners will discover if you can keep up,' she said crisply, before turning away as someone claimed her attention.

He watched her for a moment before turning back to Romana. 'No one would take the two of you for sisters,' he said. 'She's not a bit like you.'

'Not a bit,' she agreed. 'But then we have different mothers.' She removed her arm from his, lifting her smooth pale shoulders in a barely perceptible shrug. 'We all have different mothers.' Then, 'Sorry, Niall.'

'Sorry? What for?'

'She's the one with brains, class and style. I'm the one with too much hair and an out of control coffee-cup.'

She'd summed up his first impression of her in a sentence. It irritated him that she could see through him so easily, that he'd let his prejudice show.

'You've dealt with the hair,' he said.

She shrugged. 'Just a public relations exercise on behalf of our new stylist, Niall. I'm a walking advertisement for the store.' She touched her necklace. 'This is part of a new range commissioned by Flora. And even the scent is our new line. I'm afraid you picked the wrong sister.'

He caught a discordant undertone in the teasing note of her voice. Did the youngest Claibourne feel overshadowed by her clever and glamorous sibling? Was that just the tiniest hint of an inferiority complex?

'On the whole I think not. I'm sure India is best left to Jordan. I wouldn't have missed all this fun for the world.'

'Fun!' She gave him a sharp look, her brows raised in surprise.

'Isn't it meant to be fun?' And he smiled. She wasn't the only one capable of teasing.

The only surprising thing about it was that he'd thought he'd forgotten how.

Romana sat back in the car and sighed. 'One down, five more days to go.'

'You were worried?'

'Are you kidding?' She glanced at Niall as he fastened his seatbelt. 'You have no idea how many things can go wrong.'

'Like one car arriving instead of two?'

She bridled inwardly at his implied criticism. Molly had booked an extra car to collect Niall, but getting him home again appeared to have slipped through the cracks. In the kind of schedule she'd been coping with it was understandable.

'Good grief, that's nothing. I could have taken the Underground at a pinch.'

'I wouldn't advise it,' he replied. 'Not in that dress.'

Much as it pained her to admit it, he had a point. 'Called a minicab, then,' she said. 'A minor mix-up over cars for the bit-players is nothing to get worked up about. No one who matters was inconvenienced.' That was not entirely true. She wasn't at all happy at being forced to spend any 'off-duty' time in such close proximity to the man. He gave her the impression that he knew exactly what she was thinking. And *she* hadn't a clue what was going on his mind. It was just too disturbing.

'That implies that either I've not been inconvenienced or that I don't matter,' he said, taking her by surprise. She hadn't thought he was the kind of man to make a fuss over such a small detail. Maybe he was simply trying to wrongfoot her by picking her up on every little problem.

'You're my shadow,' she reminded him. 'What applies to me, applies to you.' She glanced at him, offering him the opportunity to dispute the way she viewed the situation. He didn't take it.

All evening she'd been conscious of him at her back, watching her as she'd kept one step ahead of the action, smoothing out any small wrinkle that might mar the perfection of the evening.

All evening she'd been aware of the scent he'd bought her. Subtle, elusive, indefinable. Inescapable. And, like the sudden heat in his eyes as she'd offered her wrist to him, deeply disturbing.

'To be honest, I'd have thought you'd have welcomed a little drama,' he said, wrenching her out of her thoughts. 'It would have given you a chance to demonstrate your competence in a crisis.'

He just couldn't resist it, could he? Well, she was happy enough to rise to his bait on this occasion. 'I hadn't thought of it that way.' Probably because she wasn't a complete idiot. 'I see now that I should have organised some small calamity for that very purpose. Nothing too dreadful; a mishap with a tray of hors d'oeuvres, perhaps. A drunken waiter with amorous intentions towards Her Royal Highness. My mistake. But then...' she held the pause just long enough to let him know exactly what she was thinking '...I assumed it would be the quality of the entertainment provided in conjunction with a total *lack* of drama behind the scenes that would impress you most.' She waited politely for him to admit that he was.

There was only the slightest hesitation before he said, 'I'm impressed.'

'Thank you. Now, where can I drop you?'

'I'd be more comfortable if we did it the other way around.'

'Such gallantry really isn't necessary, Niall. This isn't a date, it's business, and Claibourne & Farraday are equal-opportunity employers.' Something to stress in the present circumstances. 'Where do you want to go?'

'I live in Spitalfields,' he said, and when she hesitated, confounding herself for a fool, added, 'I thought it might be out of your way.'

Oh, it was. Miles. Which was why he'd suggested dropping her first. Not gallantry, just common sense. She was glad of the darkness in the rear of the car as she blushed for her stupid remark about it not being 'a date'. Nothing could have been further from either of their minds, so what on earth had made her say such a thing?

Tiredness, perhaps. Or hunger. She hadn't eaten since she'd snatched a bite of that sandwich mid-afternoon, and she'd been too busy to indulge in the exquisite savouries provided by the C&F caterers during the interval tonight. It was too late to regret her haste in rebuffing his thoughtfulness, and, having made such a prickly point of dropping him first, she simply nodded to the driver.

'Spitalfields, please,' she said. Then, as the car pulled smoothly away from the kerb, 'Spitalfields? Have you lived there long?'

'About four years.'

'How unexpected. I would have placed you in Kensington, or Chelsea. A small town house in one of those discreet cul-de-sacs off the King's Road, perhaps.' Anywhere but the vibrant, newly fashionable East End.

'It's convenient for the City, and the restaurants are good.' He shrugged. 'And I'm a member of the area development board.' Catching her doubtful look, he added, 'Jack the Ripper doesn't live there any more.'

'I thought that was Whitechapel,' she said, trying to recall what she knew about Spitalfields. Then, with a sudden flash of insight, 'Oh, do you live in one of the old silk-merchants' houses?' She'd seen a programme on television about the regeneration of the area. 'Eighteenth-century?' She dredged her memory. 'Built by the Huguenots, now being rescued from generations of multi-occupancy and re-gentrified?'

'The house was practically derelict when I bought it. Restoration is still very much a work in progress.' He shrugged. 'With not much progress, to be honest. Louise was part of an action group to restore the houses, and without her...' He stopped, as if that explained everything.

'Louise? She was your wife?'

'Yes. She was an architectural historian. We met when her campaign group was trying to raise finance to buy the house and restore it. So I bought it.'

She glanced at him. 'Just like that?'

'It seemed like a good investment.'

'Oh, I see.'

'And I wanted Louise to have the pleasure of restoring it. Returning it to its glory. As the owner, I was able to drop in any time.'

'Oh, I *see*. You fell in love with her.'

'The first time I saw her,' he admitted. 'A year later I gave her the house as a wedding present.'

'Before the restoration was complete?'

'I couldn't wait that long.'

'Oh, but that's so…' He glanced at her sharply. About to say romantic, she stopped herself just in time. Instead she said, 'I'm so sorry.'

He frowned. 'What for?'

'Because I'd assumed you were divorced.' She'd suddenly realised that he wasn't. 'If you're still living in the house you gave her, that's clearly not the case,' she said. Then, sensing his hesitation. 'I'm sorry. It's none of my business.'

He closed his eyes briefly, as if the memory still pained him physically, before he said,

'There's no need to apologise. She died four years ago.'

She didn't ask, but he told her anyway. Perhaps used to the tactful silence of curious strangers and wanting to get it out of the way.

'We were in the Indian Ocean. She brushed against a coral outcrop when I took her out on a reef, snorkelling.' He lifted his hands in a gesture of helplessness. 'A scratch, that's all. Nothing. She was dead within a week.'

Romana swallowed. 'I'm so sorry.' Then the time scale registered. Four years ago. He'd lived in the house for four years. He'd bought it for Louise as a wedding present. They'd been on their honeymoon.

'Hence the lack of progress,' he said. Romana felt rather than saw the suggestion of a shrug. 'She'd give me hell for not getting on with it. For not finishing what she started.'

'No!' Without thinking Romana reached out and touched his arm. 'No, really. It must be very difficult to cope with. I'm sure she'd understand.'

'Are you?' That appeared to amuse him. 'India put me very much in mind of her to-night. They share the same colouring—dark eyes and hair. The same fine bones.' He paused, looked at her without a trace of the anguish she'd been imagining. Without any emotion at all. As if he'd made a conscious decision to shut down the feeling, responsive part of himself. 'The same forthright manner,' he added.

Embarrassed by her impetuous gesture, by her desire to offer him comfort that he plainly didn't want, Romana snatched back her hand. 'In that case I hope she doesn't haunt you, or you're in deep trouble.' She realised belatedly that her gesture was the least of her worries. Her impetuous mouth had always been the problem. 'Er…I'll shut up now.'

'No, don't do that. Tell me about tomorrow. What excitement have you got in store for me?'

The dry manner in which he said that word *excitement* made her forget all about her embarrassment. If he'd been anyone else, she'd have assumed it had been deliberate.

'Excitement? You want excitement? Well, this is your lucky week. Tomorrow begins with a visit to a special-needs adventure play facility we financed with last year's fund-raising. Official opening, photographs, meet the press. Pictures of happy kids for the website.'

'All of them wearing Claibourne & Farraday sweatshirts, I have no doubt.'

'Of course. It's a PR exercise. Don't forget to bring yours.'

He gave her a look that suggested she'd be lucky. Well, India would certainly prefer it if he remained anonymous. No one would bother with some stiff-necked man in a suit, observing from the sidelines. With any luck the press would take him for someone from the Health & Safety Executive. 'That's if you decide to come,' she said. 'It's not compulsory.'

'And in the afternoon?' he asked.

'A celebrity auction at the store. Bits and bobs of the famous. Football kit signed by one the premier teams. Film stars' underwear, ditto. You know the sort of thing. If I've got it right it'll be a media madhouse.'

'You'll understand, I hope, if I leave my chequebook at home?'

'You've been more than generous already, Niall. The money will be well spent, I promise. You'll see that for yourself, tomorrow morning.'

He made no comment. 'And in the evening?' he asked.

'In the evening...' Oh, knickers! There was no way she could even *suggest* he joined in the entertainment lined up for the evening. 'Nothing,' she said quickly. 'Straight home, put my feet up, fall asleep in front of the TV. You can catch up on your decorating. Oh!' She covered her mouth with both hands.

He reached across and, taking her wrist, removed one hand from her mouth. 'Tell me, Romana...'

'Yes?'

'Are you hungry?'

'Hungry?' That was the last question she'd expected.

'You've been running around since six o'clock, making sure everyone was having a good time. The catering was lavish, but I didn't see you eat a thing. And you missed lunch.' His face bore the suggestion of a smile, but it was probably just the shadow from the streetlamps they were passing. 'I just wondered if you were hungry.'

'Because I keep putting my foot in my mouth?' she asked.

'Spitalfields coming up, sir,' the driver said.

He gave the name of the street and then turned back to her. 'Maybe...' he began, a touch hesitantly. 'Maybe you'd like to see the house? And I'll make us both some supper.'

'But it's late. The driver—'

'I'm sure he'd welcome an extra hour of overtime. If your budget will stand it?'

About to refuse—she was tired and she had no desire to get cosy over scrambled eggs with Niall Macaulay—she reconsidered. She had to take any opportunity offered to get to know the man a little better. She had a huge stake in the success of Claibourne's. All her energy, years of her life... There was no way she was going to surrender it to a banker with a ledger for a heart.

She backed away from that image. It wasn't true. He was cool...cold, even...but he hadn't always been that way. She needed to understand what made him tick, discover what might convince him to leave things as they were.

'My budget is well in hand,' she said, then swallowed a yawn and glanced at the driver. 'Would that be all right? Can you come back in an hour?'

'Yes, ma'am,' he said.

Niall led the way up a small flight of steps and unlocked the front door. He switched on a light and stood back to let her inside. The half-panelling in the hall had long ago been painted in the kind of green that was now packaged and sold expensively as a "heritage" colour, then decorated with free-form flowers and foliage, much faded but still lovely.

'This is original?' she asked, astonished.

'Yes. Fortunately it had been boarded over. There's a room upstairs, too, where we found the original decoration beneath some old wall-paper. I'll give you the tour later, but we'll eat first. Come through to the kitchen; it's warm in there.'

He indicated an aged sofa pushed back against the far wall of a large and comfortable kitchen. There was nothing stainless steel and modern about it. Nothing fancy. It was the sort of kitchen where a dozen or more people might gather, after a hard day of doing whatever architectural historians and restorers did, to eat and drink and talk into the night.

And, when everyone else had gone home, the sofa was big enough for two.

'Make yourself at home—put your feet up while I warm some of C&F's finest ''home-made'' soup.'

'Well?' Jordan enquired. 'How was your first day shadowing Romana Claibourne?'

'Interesting. And long.' He yawned.

'You spent the evening with her?'

'Only in the line of duty.' Niall looked at the silver-framed photograph on the dressing table, saw Louise's sweet face smiling up him.

Duty had ceased the minute the car drew up in front of his house, he knew. And it was Louise's house. He'd never invited another woman across the threshold. To rest on her sofa. Eat from her plates.

But Romana had looked pale and tired and he'd been sure she wouldn't take the trouble to eat when she got home. Of course it was entirely possible that there would have been someone there ready to put a hot cup of cocoa into her hands before tucking her up in bed. But she'd said yes, which suggested not. Maybe.

Maybe she'd just been taking the opportunity to get beneath his skin, find out what made him tick. He tried to convince himself that that was what he'd been doing. It wasn't true. He hadn't wanted to say goodnight.

He stared at Louise's photograph, trying to wipe out the image of Romana that intruded between them, feeling the dull ache of guilt that every day Louise was a little fainter, a little further from him. Then he laid the photograph down, unable to bear what now seemed to be only reproach.

'Duty?' Jordan prompted. 'Were you at the charity gala? I caught it on the late-evening news. I didn't see you in the line-up to be presented to royalty.'

'Neither was Romana. She was behind the scenes, ensuring everything ran like clockwork.' Niall tucked the telephone beneath his ear as he unfastened his cuff-links. 'I was at her side. Observing.'

'So?'

'It was a highly successful evening. Well-organised and very entertaining. Romana Claibourne is not quite as dizzy as she looks.' She hadn't fluffed her hair once during the entire evening. Well, not intentionally anyway. Once or twice he'd seen her make a move to twist a curl, only to realise belatedly that there was nothing to twist. He found himself smiling at the way her pretty new haircut had framed her face as she'd slept. The smile faded as he recalled the silk of her skin beneath his fingers.

'Pity,' Jordan said, reclaiming his wandering attention.

'No, the pity is that you weren't there, too. India looked every inch the chief executive,' he said provokingly as he tugged at his tie, releasing a ghost of the scent Romana had been wearing. He lifted it to his face to catch the lingering traces, recalling the way she'd held out her wrist to him. Recalling the way her hand had felt in his as he'd taken it from her mouth after her tongue had run away with her. Not *quite* as dizzy as she looked. Well, that would be impossible. Just *averagely* dizzy. 'You should have been at her side.'

'India Claibourne will keep,' Jordan said sharply. 'What are you doing tomorrow?'

He grimaced at the phone. 'I'm on playground duty.' Where the playground was, he realised belatedly, he had no idea. Unsurprisingly, Romana had omitted to tell him. He'd have to phone the store first thing. Ask Molly to fax him through the programme for the rest of the week. He did have business of his own to fit in somehow... 'Shadowing isn't all balance sheets and boardrooms.' Then, changing the subject, 'I took a look around the store this afternoon. You're right. It needs ripping out and refitting from top to bottom.'

'Of course it does.' Distracted by his hobby-horse, Jordan forgot all about playgrounds. 'Peter Claibourne has been living in the past. Worse, he's been neglecting the future.'

'Maybe he knows more than you think. It'll be an expensive business,' Niall warned.

'Progress is never cheap. Keep in touch.'

CHAPTER FIVE

'WELL?' India demanded, the minute they'd left the traffic of London behind them. 'Tell me about Niall Macaulay. What's he like?'

What was he like? All through the night Romana had been wrestling a maelstrom of confusing impressions. Coldness. Cleverness. A sarcastic misogynist who thought women should be seen and not heard—and he wasn't even too sure about the 'seen'. A man of stunning presence, who could turn a woman's head without raising a sweat. A man it would give her enormous pleasure to bring to his knees and force to admit that she was his equal. She'd been so sure she had the man taped. And then, in a heartbeat, he'd overthrown all her opinions by telling her about his wife.

'What's he *after*?' India demanded.

'What? Oh…' Romana was certain of only one thing. That Niall Macaulay had no interest in running a department store, no matter how grand it was. Since she preferred to be driven by someone whose mind was entirely on the task, she wasn't about to tell her sister that. Instead she said, 'Please, Indie! Keep your eyes on the road. And slow down!'

India glanced at her. 'What's up with you this morning?'

'Nothing.' Just a firm belief that she'd lived dangerously enough for one week. 'I didn't get much sleep last night, that's all.'

India glanced at her again, this time with sympathy. 'I haven't slept properly since the lawyers dropped the ''golden share'' bombshell. So, tell me, what happened last night?'

'Last night? Nothing happened last night!' As her sister's head swivelled, her 'trouble' antennae now on full alert, Romana realised she'd said it too quickly, too emphatically.

'Not so much as a dropped tray. I was just too wound up to sleep. Or tense, maybe. I seemed to spend the entire night reliving that moment when I jumped into space. Bouncing up and down.' She felt queasy just thinking

about it. Which served her right for being eco-
nomical with the truth.

'You didn't have to do it, Ro.'

'Didn't I?' She shrugged. 'Maybe not. It
made all the newspapers this morning, though.
Even the broadsheets.'

'I saw. It would have been quite brilliant if
it hadn't been for Niall Macaulay with his arm
around your shoulders under the headline
''Claibourne and Farraday Jump for JOY''.
Whatever were you thinking about?'

'I thought I'd impress him with my PR
skills. As you said, it made all the newspapers.'

'It provoked speculation about the Farradays
in the morning papers,' India grumbled. 'Made
them noticeable. I don't even want to hear that
name, Romana. I certainly don't want to read
it.'

'It's difficult to avoid,' she said, trying to
make light of it, trying not to remember the
way she'd felt when he'd stood at her side, her
body pressed tightly against his. 'Since it's
over the front door.'

'Not for much longer. Once this nonsense is sorted I'm going to rebrand the store and change the name to Claibourne's.' She turned to Romana. 'Sharp, snappy and modern. What do you think?'

Romana stared at her sister's determined profile and realised she'd had this all worked out. She'd probably been working on it for years. No wonder she was so mad at Jordan Farraday for throwing a spanner in her carefully oiled works.

'I think,' she replied, carefully, 'that you shouldn't even be thinking that, let alone saying it out loud. Have you told anyone else?'

'No. It's between you and me for now.'

And she'd rather not have known. 'Keep it that way. In fact I think you should forget all about it, put it out of your head until you're in a position to make it happen. Believe me, if Jordan Farraday finds out what you're planning...' She didn't think she had to spell it out, but her sister's face was set in stubborn mode. 'Promise me, Indie.'

'All right! Just keep them out of the news.'

'I'll do my best,' she promised. But she wasn't offering any guarantees.

She'd spent weeks setting up publicity to ensure a high profile for the store during charity week. Now she'd opened Pandora's box, and the Farradays would be fools if they didn't use it to their own advantage. She didn't know about his cousins, but she was quite certain that Niall Macaulay wasn't a fool.

India lifted one hand from the steering wheel in a gesture of apology. 'The store is more important than some stupid inter-family feud that's been simmering for a hundred and fifty years. I'm hoping the Farradays can be made to see the sense of leaving things the way they are—'

'Hardly likely if they find out you're planning to take their name from above the front door.'

'If we do end up in court we can at least show that we're competent, successful, forward-thinking.'

'Competent isn't a problem. Successful...' She shrugged. 'Niall is well aware that sales haven't been exactly buoyant in the last couple of years. As for forward-thinking...' While their father had left the day-to-day running of the store to India for years—the only reason things weren't a lot worse—he had stubbornly resisted the modernisation plans she'd commissioned, insisting that the attraction of the store lay in its time-warp atmosphere. It was certainly great for encouraging tourists, but they were running a store, not a heritage site.

'I don't need you quoting Niall Macaulay at me,' India snapped, betraying her own unease. 'Just make sure that he sees us as an unbeatable combination.'

'I'll certainly try.' Romana thought it better not to mention that while Niall had been heating up soup, giving her a potted history of his house, she'd fallen asleep on the sofa in his warm kitchen. That he'd woken her only when the car arrived to take her home.

She'd come from a deep, deep sleep, not sure where she was, and the first thing she'd seen was his face as he leaned over her, had been aware only of his hand on her shoulder.

And for a moment she'd seen someone other than the dour, cold man who'd been dogging her footsteps all day. Someone she might like. More than like.

Great impression she must have made on him. From the haste with which he'd removed his hand she just knew that she'd snored. Or dribbled. Probably both.

She emitted an involuntary mew of delayed embarrassment.

Her sister glanced at her. 'What?'

'Nothing. Just something in my throat.' She made a point of clearing it.

At least she wouldn't have to face him this morning. She'd never got around to telling him the location of the adventure playground they were opening. And he hadn't asked. Presumably he didn't find the prospect of twenty or so sets of sticky fingers grabbing at his perfectly creased trousers especially appealing.

Smart man, she thought as India turned into the car park, slotting her Mercedes coupé between a black Aston Martin convertible and the Mayoral Rolls. The guests were prompt, at least.

Maybe Niall would give the celebrity auction a miss, too. He hadn't looked too impressed by the idea, and he must have pressing concerns of his own to deal with. There was no way he could spend every minute of the working day at her back. Which should have been comforting. But oddly wasn't. His ascerbic remarks seemed to set her up, give life an edge...

She left India talking to a group of local VIPs and headed for the big log cabin built to provide a warm, safe environment for indoor play. Today it was also stacked with supplies of free goodies, including the sweatshirts so despised by Niall, and tenanted by the caterers booked to provide refreshments for both adults and children.

Molly was already there with some of her staff, making sure that the C&F flags were flying the right way up and the banner was straight. She'd also grabbed all spare hands to fix bunches of balloons to anything that was fastened down. One of the spare hands, she realised—a fraction too late to get her face under control—belonged to Niall Macaulay. No prizes for guessing who'd come in the Aston, then. Dark, dangerous and sexy, it suited him down to the ground. He straightened as she approached.

'Niall, I didn't expect to see you here.'

'I've been here since ten-thirty—which, according to the schedule, is when you should have arrived.'

'Blame India,' Molly said. And from behind Niall's back she winked. 'She's such a sedate driver. Nothing will persuade her to go over fifty, even on the motorway.'

Romana pulled her lips hard back against her teeth to stop herself from breaking out in hysterical laughter. Whether at Molly's outrageous lie or at the sight of Niall wearing jeans and a Claibourne & Farraday sweatshirt.

The jeans, she couldn't help but notice, clung to his thighs in the most photogenic manner, and his hair looked as if it had been recently combed with his fingers. Nothing could have been further from the image that had so impressed itself upon her only twenty-four hours earlier.

'Schedule?' she asked, forcing herself to keep her mind on the job. 'What schedule? I didn't even give you the location of the play-ground. I don't believe you actually asked...'

Niall wasn't fooled. She'd hoped to evade him this morning. He didn't blame her, but this game was being played to win and he didn't plan on coming in as runner-up. 'I rang your office first thing. You weren't there.' He waited for some response, then, when none was forthcoming, 'Of course you did have a very late night,' he added, as if that explained it.

Her cheeks flushed a particularly fetching shade of pink. 'For your information,' she declared, 'I was at the Savoy at seven-thirty this morning, ensuring everything was under control for this evening's fashion—' She stopped, horrified at the gaffe she'd just made. 'Show,' she finished lamely.

In her haste to correct any suspicion that she'd been lying in bed until ten o'clock, she'd let slip that which she'd been at such pains to hide. That far from being at home with her feet up in front of the TV tonight, she'd be preventing mass hysteria behind the scenes at a full-scale fashion show.

In other words, she'd lied to him.

'Would that be the Wedding and Honeymoon Fashion Show?' he asked, just in case she was in any doubt that he knew she'd lied to him. 'Molly kindly faxed me an entire list of the week's activities,' he explained, before she could answer. 'Despite all appearances to the contrary, I do have a business life of my own to fit around yours.'

'I'm sorry,' she said. Well, there really wasn't anything else she could say. She'd lied. He knew she'd lied. She knew he knew... 'I really didn't think you'd want to come.'

'No?'

Holding the list of events in his hands that morning, Niall had known exactly what she'd been thinking. But he neither wanted nor needed her sympathy. That he wanted something was evident from the fact he'd cut through management waffle this morning and a meeting that had been scheduled to last all morning had been got through in an hour. Just so he could be here. At the time he'd told himself it was essential for the Farraday claim that he kept a close eye on Romana Claibourne. The minute he'd set eyes on her, he'd known he was fooling himself.

'I just thought...'

'Tell me,' he said, stopping her before she told him why she'd decided not to burden him with a fashion show dedicated to weddings and honeymoons, 'did you manage to get more than the hour's sleep you snatched at my place? When you finally got home this morning?'

Molly's mouth dropped open in a most satisfactory way. And from Romana's expression he'd effectively dealt with any warm feeling she might be harbouring towards him.

'One of your balloons is escaping,' was her only response, and the chill emanating from her was like opening a refrigerator door.

Mission accomplished. Keep it impersonal. Keep it distant.

No more late-night suppers. No more touching.

Grabbing Molly by the arm, Romana dragged her into the cabin. 'Don't say a word,' she hissed. Molly opened her mouth. 'Not one! I fell asleep on his sofa, all right? This is business, pure and simple, so you can stow your lurid imagination. He was just being pathetically *male*.'

Which, on reflection, surprised her. Even supposing something *had* happened between them, Niall wasn't the kind of man to chalk his conquests on the men's room wall. So had he chosen, quite deliberately, to annoy her? He must have anticipated her reaction, so why would he do that when he had the most to gain by being friendly, winning her trust? She shook her head. Fat chance of that happening.

Seeing that Molly would burst if she didn't say what was on her mind, she said, 'Oh, for goodness' sake, speak before you go pop.'

'I have just one question.'

'Well?'

'What were you doing on his sofa?'

Niall put his head around the door. 'A television crew from the local station is looking for you, and a busload of kids have just arrived. I thought you'd probably want to know.'

'Saved by the bus...' Molly murmured.

'Just bring those sweatshirts.'

'Can I do anything to help?' Niall asked.

Romana wasn't impressed. He'd shown his true colours and she knew now that her first impression of the man had been spot-on. Right now his eagerness was only to see her make a fool of herself for him all over again: this time with the television cameras rolling.

'Stick to what you came for, Niall. To watch and learn. Just keep from under my feet while you're doing it.' She didn't wait for a response, but went in search of the TV crew to brief them about getting pictures of India cutting the ribbon to open the play facility and ensure they got plenty of pictures of happy kids having fun.

As if that wasn't enough, she also had to ensure that they didn't get any of the pretender to the boardroom of Claibourne & Farraday.

Niall decided he'd be more usefully occupied helping the children into their sweatshirts, but couldn't take his gaze off Romana as she handed out press packs, answered questions, introduced India and one of the local worthies to journalists. Seemingly doing a dozen things at once without looking in the slightest bit flustered. It was a master-class in keeping calm under pressure.

Whether it was genuine calm, or she was simply keeping a tight lid on her feelings, it was impressive.

A child tugged at his jeans for attention and held up her sweatshirt. He folded himself to child height to help her find her way into the sleeves.

'Romana told me she fell asleep on your sofa,' Molly said as she passed out the shirts.

'Did I suggest anything else?'

'I think you know exactly what you were suggesting. I must say you're something of a disappointment. I hoped for much better when I fixed it so that you'd have to go home together.'

The one thing that had gone wrong during the whole evening had been deliberately set up by Romana's PA? Why, for heaven's sake? Surely Romana Claibourne had men falling over themselves for the privilege of taking her home. Taking her anywhere she wanted to go.

'Our relationship is purely business, Molly,' he said firmly. And ignored the seductive memory of Romana's skin beneath his fingers. Her sweetness in trying to protect him from painful reminders of Louise. Kindness that he'd rejected... But he was still here.

'Romana said that, too.' The child flung her arms around his neck and he stood up with her, looking around for her carer. 'It doesn't have to be that way,' Molly added. 'And, speaking personally, I think you should ask her out to lunch to make up for your total lack of gallantry this morning.'

'Speaking personally,' he replied, 'I think she'd tell me what to do with lunch.' But the idea, once planted, was immovably attractive. 'However, if you book a table at the Weston Arms, I'll see if I can tempt her.'

'Consider it done.'

At that moment, however, Romana was busy fixing up a ribbon for the official opening. As if sensing his gaze, she glanced up. Her expression suggested she wasn't convinced by his involvement. And that lunch was unlikely.

Romana pinned the ribbons in place, then concentrated very hard on tying large bows with trailing ribbons at each end. But, despite promising herself that she wouldn't look in his direction, she still found her gaze drawn to Niall as he stood among the mothers and helpers, encouraging the children, keeping a watchful eye on them.

There was nothing of the hard-edged businessman about him as he chatted to the carers, provided a steady hand as needed. And she couldn't fail to notice the way he drew the eyes of every woman in the place.

Any other time, any other circumstances, and she knew she'd be looking too.

'Romana…' She turned as someone grabbed her arm. 'We've got a problem in the kitchen.'

'What kind of problem?' She glanced towards Niall. The *Celebrity* magazine photographer was prowling in his direction and she made a move to cut him off.

'The kind that won't wait.'

'Mr Farraday?' It was the *Celebrity* magazine photographer who'd been at the bungee-jump. 'I'd like a photograph of you with the children, if you don't mind.' Niall glanced in Romana's direction, expecting her to put a stop to his photo opportunity. But she'd disappeared.

'Sure,' he said.

'I don't believe this!' Romana, kneeling in two inches of water, was in a mood to murder a plumber. The stopcock was wet and slippery and she couldn't get a grip on it. And the stupid girl she'd asked for a cloth had rushed off like a headless chicken and hadn't come back. In desperation Romana pulled off her sweatshirt and used that. Gradually the stopcock began to move. Soaked through and thoroughly chilled, she couldn't tell whether anything was happening at the business end. 'Someone— anyone,' she shouted, 'is it stopping?'

'Problem?'

She bit back an expletive as Niall crouched down beside her. 'No, I do this for fun.'

'Oh, right.' He made a move to go. 'I'll leave you to it, then—'

'No!' She instinctively put out her hand, grasping his warm wrist to keep him at her side. 'I'm sorry, I didn't mean to snap. The tap came off in the caterer's hand.' The sudden quiet at least assured her that the water had stopped gushing all over the kitchen. She realised that she was gripping his wrist like a drowning woman clinging to a life raft. 'Niall…about last night.' She expected him to say, Forget it. You were tired. Something like that. He didn't say a word. 'I shouldn't have

snapped at you when I arrived. I was just...
well, I felt...'

'Embarrassed?'

'Yes. I don't normally fall asleep when
someone asks me to supper.'

'I'm sure you were tired.'

That might have done the trick if he hadn't
made it sound less like reassurance and more
as if she'd been living it up instead of working
day and night to make the JOY campaign a
huge success.

'I've been working long hours,' she retali-
ated defensively. Then, because this was supposed to be an apology, she tried again. 'And
I shouldn't have lied about the fashion show.
I just didn't think you'd want to...' She faltered. It was so much easier to say exactly
what she thought when she wasn't thinking.

'Want to shadow you at a fashion show?'

'No. At least not that fashion show. I didn't
want to...'

'Bring up the past?'

'I don't suppose it ever goes away, does it?'

'No.' Then, 'Did you know you snore? Very gently. Like a little piglet...'

She snatched her hand back, unravelled her soaking sweatshirt from around the stopcock.

'What is it about stopcocks?' she demanded, returning to the safer subject of plumbing. 'Do plumbers get a kick out of tightening them to immovability, do you suppose? Or is it just to guarantee that feeble women have to pay their outrageous call-out charges?'

'Sound business practice—if you're a plumber,' he said. 'I'll find a mop.' Niall straightened, so that she was left with a full-frontal view of his denim-clad thighs. 'And a bucket.' She backed carefully out of the sink-unit cupboard, trying not to cause a wave, and stood up. 'You get out of those wet things.'

'For goodness' sake, Niall, a bit of water won't kill me.' She started opening cupboards, looking for the mop.

'Here, take this,' he said, pulling his sweat-shirt over his head, ruffling his hair even more, and handing it to her.

'Don't fuss,' she said, resisting the urge to take it, warm from his body, and wrap it about her.

'I'm not fussing. Trust me on this, Romana. You really need to get out of those wet things. Now.' And, pushing the sweatshirt into her hands, he backed her in the direction of the cloakroom.

'But—'

'But nothing. I may not know a lot about PR, but you can safely leave me to deal with a flooded floor.'

CHAPTER SIX

ROMANA deeply resented Niall's high-handedness, but she didn't have time to argue so she took the sweatshirt and retreated through the lobby and into the Ladies'.

Then she turned and faced her reflection in the mirror.

And groaned.

Her white silk shirt was soaked through and transparent. As was the lace bra beneath it. She might as well have been naked.

She knew she should be grateful that Niall hadn't just left her to find out for herself when she opened the pages of *Celebrity* magazine, because the photographer wouldn't have missed an opportunity like that. He'd have made a great story out of 'How Romana Saved the Day'. And she'd have had to just grin and—she pulled a face—bear it.

She stripped off her blouse and bra, rolled them up and stuffed them into her bag. Then she dried herself and her hair, which had taken a full-frontal soaking before she'd been able to get beneath the sink. Only then did she pull on Niall's sweatshirt.

It felt soft and warm against her skin, and it smelled good. There was leather and fresh air and something indefinable that was Niall Macaulay. She didn't have time to analyse it, though. The caterers needed the kitchen. So she flung open the door, prepared to resume battle with the mop.

It wasn't necessary. Niall had used a wet-and-dry vacuum to suck up the water. The floor was dry. Disaster averted. He wasn't even breathing hard. She muttered something short and scatological beneath her breath.

'Okay?' he said, straightening from the cupboard where he was stowing the machine.

'Er, yes. Thank you. You've done a great job. And thanks for this,' she said, pulling at the front of the sweatshirt.

'My pleasure.'

'I don't doubt it.' She wasn't usually coy, or given to blushing, but she really wished she hadn't said that. Looking around, anywhere but at him, she quickly went on, 'I don't know where Molly's girls have disappeared to.'

'Maybe they didn't want to get their feet wet.' The corner of his mouth kinked in the suggestion of a smile.

'While you're getting used to it?' she responded, finally meeting his gaze head-on.

'You're a dangerous lady to get close to,' he agreed, but he was smiling as he said it.

'We're three dangerous ladies,' she replied sharply. 'Warn your partners.' Then, 'I'd better go and let the caterers know that it's safe to return.'

'Leave it a minute or two while I fix the tap.'

'You can do that?'

'Watch and learn,' he told her. Just as she'd advised him. Then, 'You learn fast when you live in an old house. Something's always coming away in your hand.'

'Oh, right.' She tucked her damp curls behind her ears. 'Well, I'd better go and make sure nothing else has gone wrong,' she said. She turned in the doorway. He was already bent over the sink but she couldn't leave it like that. 'Thanks for your help,' she said again. And, because she knew she'd been churlish, 'This has to be above and beyond the call of shadowdom.'

Niall straightened, and all trace of a smile had disappeared. 'Just what did you expect, Romana? That I'd stand back and watch you struggle? Make notes, perhaps? Award you marks out of ten for the way you handled the situation? The speed with which you reacted? Taking points off for bad language?'

'Of course not!' She looked shocked at his angry response. He was rather shocked himself. Shocked that she could have thought him so cold. He hadn't used to be cold. 'I didn't mean—'

'Didn't you? Those kids are more important than our petty squabbles. A lot more important than faulty plumbing fixing,' he said, and meant it. But it didn't change anything else. 'Of course, if it had happened in the store—' he shrugged '—I'd be less inclined to overlook the matter.'

'I see. So why aren't you there with a team of surveyors, checking the maintenance records? Why are you here at a very small, very local adventure playground for special-needs children?'

She had a point. He wasn't learning anything about running a national institution out here in the sticks. But he was learning a lot about Romana Claibourne. None of which Jordan would want to hear.

'Getting you out of a fix?' he offered.

'Romana, I've got to get back to town. Legal stuff.' India glanced in the direction of Niall Macaulay, who was talking to Molly. Then, 'Was he impressed, do you think?'

'Impressed?' He put out his hand and touched Molly's arm, smiling as he said good-bye, and Romana felt a sharp stab of something very like jealousy at the easy manner between them.

'Romana?'

'What? Oh...' She dragged her thoughts back from the brink of that particular no-go area and decided that this was not a good moment to tell her sister how he'd saved the day. There never would be a good moment... 'He's hardly likely to say so, is he?'

'I suppose not,' India said as she climbed into her car.

Niall looked up, as if sensing that he was being talked about, and with a final word to Molly headed towards them.

'Keep a close eye on him, Romana. He was talking to that photographer from *Celebrity* magazine the minute your back was turned.'

He joined her as India reversed briskly out of her parking space with the minimum of effort, before heading out towards the main road. 'You're going to need a ride back to town,' he said.

'I'll go with Molly.'

'She anticipated that. She's a bit pressed for room so she asked me if I'd give you a lift. She said she'll see you at the auction.'

Romana groaned. 'I'm not going to survive today, let alone the week.' She glanced at her watch. 'How soon can we get back to town?'

'She also said I was to make sure you had a proper lunch.'

Her assistant, she decided, was getting entirely too bossy. She didn't want to think about the surge of pleasure on learning that Molly's tête-à-tête with Niall had been on her behalf.

'Thanks shadow-man, but I'm a big girl. You can take it as read that I know how to use a knife and fork. I'm sure your bank needs you more than I do right now.'

'I put in a day's work between five and nine-thirty this morning. And bankers, like public relations directors, have to eat.'

'I really do need to get back to work.'

'I have my instructions. Give you a lift, give you lunch and apologise.'

'Apologise? What for?'

'Apparently I failed ''gallantry'' this morning,' he said. He indicated his car. 'If you've got everything?' Since she had her roomy carryall bag over her shoulder, she could hardly deny it. 'Then let's go.' He pressed the remote on his keyring to unlock the car and then, as an afterthought, offered her the keys. 'Maybe you should drive.'

'Why?'

'A shadow is a passive thing.'

Passive? This man had never been passive in his life. The way he'd taken control of the kitchen disaster had shown him in his true colours. But she looked from the keys to the gleaming Aston Martin. 'I suspect that offer was made through gritted teeth,' she said. Then, much as she would have liked to see him sweat, she let him off the hook. 'Don't worry, Niall, your lovely car is quite safe from me. I don't have motor insurance.'

'You don't have a car?' Niall opened the door for her, and as she ducked quickly past him he seemed to catch a faint trace of the scent he'd bought her. Briefly her softly pleated trousers were moulded to her thighs, hips, as she settled into the seat, fastening the seatbelt.

The seatbelt divided her breasts, emphasising them beneath the oversized sweatshirt, and it was hard not to remember how they'd looked with the thin, transparent silk clinging wetly to them. Hard not to think about her naked beneath the sweatshirt *he'd* been wearing. It was almost like touching her.

She was so utterly female, he thought. Her curves soft and inviting. His mind filled in the silk of her skin beneath his hand and his body responded with an urgency that left him gasping.

He realised she was looking up at him, a tiny frown creasing the space between her vivid eyes, as if she was waiting for a reply to something she'd said.

'Sorry, what did you say?'

'That it's not compulsory. Owning a car.'

'Compulsory?' He was stunned at the way his mind was running, the fantasies it was conjuring up from nowhere, as if Louise had never

existed. 'Oh, no. I just assumed a smart little
town car from Daddy would have been parked
at the doorstep for your seventeenth birthday,'
he said. 'Something small and sexy. In
lipstick-pink.' She looked great in pink lipstick. Though she hadn't retouched it since
she'd arrived this morning.

Her soft, pouting lips looked great without
it, he decided. And discovered that such
thoughts were no help at all.

'Oh, I see. One of those important mile-
stones in growing up. Sex for my sixteenth
birthday, a car for my seventeenth and a drink
for my eighteenth.'

'I didn't say that.' But he'd implied it. He
shouldn't be having this conversation. He
shouldn't have come today. This wasn't shadowing; it had nothing to do with business.

She shrugged. 'It's always seemed a rather
odd arrangement of priorities to me.'

'I imagine it's more a question of bowing to
the inevitable.'

'You think so?' Her lips tucked up in a tiny,
catlike smile. 'Oh, well, two out of three isn't
bad.'

Oh, no, he wasn't going there. He didn't even want to think about that. 'Well, as you say, it's not obligatory.' And he started the car.

Which two?

'Of course I do have a driver's licence. Somewhere. And you're right about the car— except that it was red, not pink—but I've lived in London all my life. Driving in the city is a layer of stress I can do without.'

'Are you telling me you sent it back?' He reversed out of his parking space and headed for the road.

'Of course not. That would have been ungracious. I gave it to someone who actually needed a car.'

He glanced at her. She had this knack of saying and doing things to make him look at her. 'Your father didn't object?'

'Why should he? It was my car.' She was shaking her fingers through her curls in a vain attempt to get them back in some kind of order. 'He didn't say anything. I don't suppose he even noticed.'

She wasn't being deliberately shocking. She wasn't really thinking about what she'd said. But he had the feeling that she'd just exposed a very small part of her private self. He doubted that she'd meant to, and he didn't press it. He didn't want to get involved with her on that level. On any level. This was business, he reminded himself. Just business.

'Well, that's a refreshingly different attitude,' he said.

She took out a compact and retouched her lipstick. 'You're not going to try and convert me?' she asked, glancing at him sideways through ridiculously long lashes, and he suddenly caught on to the 'girly' stuff. It was deliberate, he realised. She did it when she wanted to annoy him.

'Why would I do that?' he asked, deciding that a little payback was in order. 'One less woman on the roads can only be a matter for rejoicing.'

She pulled a face. 'I was beginning to think you were thawing into a human being, Niall Macaulay.'

He thought meltdown was probably a closer analogy. He might be naturally immune to the sex-kitten image. But make that a sex kitten with brains, charm, a steely core of determination to win at any cost...

'Don't let the jeans fool you.'

She glanced across at them, her gaze lingering for a moment before she said, 'I like the jeans.'

Never had he felt so self-conscious about what he was wearing, but, since that was clearly her aim, he resisted the urge to reply in kind and they drove in silence until he indicated left at an approaching junction.

'Where are we going?'

'To get lunch,' Niall replied. 'I've got a table at the Weston Arms.'

'You don't mean that place down by the river?'

'Don't I?'

'I do hope not. Look at us!' And quite suddenly she laughed. A soft, throaty chuckle that would have melted permafrost. 'Jeans, an open-necked shirt and enough sticky fingerprints to set up a glue factory. And that's just you.' She brushed her hand over her trousers. 'And look at these poor things!' He tried very hard not to. He failed. The fine linen had dried out quickly enough, but it was now creased, with grubby patches on the knees. 'And my hair.'

'It doesn't look any different to me.' Not true. Her wild tumble of curls had been thoroughly tamed by the hairdresser for the previous night's gala. His efforts hadn't survived her doze on his sofa, and the soaking had finished the job, so that it now curled softly about her ears and into the enticing hollow at the nape of her neck.

'Forget it, Niall. They wouldn't let either of us inside the front door.'

He jerked his mind back from the void.

'You may have a point.' Lunch in a romantic riverside restaurant was the last thing he should be contemplating. Molly was one tricky lady.

'There's no ''may'' about it. Besides, I don't have time to do lunch at the Weston full justice. It's a leisurely occasion there.'

'Is it? I've never been there at lunch-time.'
The point scoring was petty. But irresistible.

'You should try it one Sunday.'

He refused to bite. He wasn't going to the
Weston with her now or at any other time.
'Maybe you'd better call and cancel the reservation.' He indicated the carphone. After
she'd done that, he said, 'Have you any idea
where we might eat without causing eyebrows
to be lifted and noses to wrinkle in disdain?'

'There's a drive-thru burger place by the
next roundabout.'

'So?'

She grinned. 'So, after this morning I crave
the artery-hardening comfort of a double-
decker cheeseburger with large fries.'

'Followed by the nerve-jangling caffeine
high of a large cola, no doubt?'

'Total bliss. Lead me to it.'

'I don't know about bliss, but I guess it
beats making polite small talk over starched
linen.'

'Polite?' She feigned surprise. 'You'd
planned on being polite? Maybe I should have
taken the restaurant option after all.'

'Too late,' he said, turning into the drive-thru. He stopped by the window, placed their order, paid, and then, after picking up the food, pulled into a parking bay so that they could eat.

'Well, this is different,' he said, opening the brown paper sack and handing Romana her lunch.

She opened the box containing her burger, picked it up and then, licking at some sauce that had dribbled onto her finger, said, 'There's a lot to be said for fast food. I'd have been chewing through the table leg by the time we'd been served at the Weston...fine restaurant though it is.' As she bit into the bun everything oozed out of the sides, involving a lot more finger-licking. 'Oh, yes... This is soooo good.'

There was a natural earthiness about her that was utterly compelling, and Niall found it an effort to drag his gaze from her fingers. She had tiny hands, slender fingers, nails painted the same vivid pink as her lips. No rings. Not even for fun. Some mayonnaise dribbled down her thumb and it was all he could do to restrain himself from taking her hand and sucking it clean.

'Maybe we could try something more civilised after the fashion show?' he suggested. 'Maybe, since we'll be at the Savoy, we could have supper in the grill?'

'You're a glutton for punishment.' She glanced sideways at him. 'Don't you think you'll have had enough of me by then?'

'Maybe you have other plans?' he enquired, side-stepping the question of just how much of her company he could take and at the same time offering her a graceful get-out. Or the chance to show that she was running scared. She took neither.

'You've got to be kidding. I haven't any time to spare for a social life this week.'

'It wouldn't be social,' he pointed out. 'We'd be working. It would be subsistence. Fully tax-deductible.'

Which certainly put her in her place. 'Thanks, but we're not doing that well on the food front. I wouldn't want to fall asleep with my face in the food.' She still wanted to get to know him better, find out what made him tick. What he was really after… She wouldn't do that in some anonymous restaurant where, with the table between them, he could keep her at a distance both physically and mentally. 'I really would like to see the rest of your house some time, though.'

'You're suggesting we try supper again?'

He couldn't resist reminding her of that, could he?

'Er… I don't think so—' Romana caught sight of the dashboard clock and gave a little yelp. 'We have to go.' She stuffed the remains of their impromptu picnic into the brown paper sack, sucked the sauce off her thumb and wiped her hands on a paper napkin. 'I'll just get rid of this.'

'Wait.' She turned to take the napkin he was holding, but instead he leaned towards her and, catching the back of her head in his palm, gently wiped the corner of her mouth with it. Then he turned her chin with the tips of his fingers and did it again on the other side.

For a moment his stone-grey eyes seemed to soften, warm, become the eyes she'd seen as he'd woken her last night—in the split second before he'd reverted to the iceman. She caught her breath, held it as the look went on, and on until she was certain that he was going to kiss her. Her lips heated up and she knew she wanted him to kiss her. Instead he released her chin and held up the napkin between two long, slender fingers. 'Mayo,' he said, before tucking the napkin into the bag.

Romana scrambled out of the car and dumped the bag in the nearest bin. Mayo! She took a deep breath—another mistake since, instead of a head-clearing blast, she filled her lungs with air tainted by the smell of burgers and traffic fumes from the nearby dual carriageway.

How could this get any worse? She'd thought he was going to kiss her—worse, had wanted him to kiss her—when all he'd been doing was mopping up the mayo that had squidged all over her face. The second time that day he'd stopped her from looking stupid.

And what had he seen in her eyes?

A reflection of what she'd seen in his?

She hadn't imagined that. And the thought made her skin prickle with excitement.

She returned to the car, concentrated on fastening her seatbelt as Niall started the engine, looking anywhere but at him. Then, as he began to move off, she said, 'I'd advise putting the top down.'

'It's not exactly mid-summer.'

'No, but it's fine and dry. Of course if you're happy for your car to smell of burgers and fries for the next week...' She shrugged. Why should she worry?

She resisted the urge to rub at her cheek. Scrub away the stirring sensation where he'd touched her. *Mayo!* No wonder he'd changed his mind about that kiss. As she let slip an involuntary mew of embarrassment, Niall glanced at her.

'Nothing,' she said quickly.

He looked doubtful, but didn't press it. 'Have you got a scarf?' he asked.

'Don't you know that men who drive convertibles are supposed to keep a supply in the glove compartment for the use of the women in their life?'

Appalled that she'd stooped to such blatant probing, she didn't wait for him to tell her that there were no women in his life. She didn't want to hear that. Instead, she opened the glove compartment and checked for herself. It contained nothing but a small first-aid box and a torch. Not so much as a hairpin to suggest that a woman had ever been in the car and marked the territory as her own.

She tutted, but with a warm little spot somewhere deep inside. 'Not one,' she said.

'Scarves or women?' he asked. Well, it wouldn't take Freud to analyse that little performance. Then he shrugged. 'I guess I'll just have to invest in an air-freshener.'

'There's no need for that.' She took a long chiffon scarf from her bag and wound it around her hair. 'I didn't say I didn't have one. Just that you should be prepared.'

By way of reply, he hit the button that folded down the roof.

CHAPTER SEVEN

DRIVING with the hood down had the advantage of precluding conversation. It didn't stop her from thinking about that nearly kiss, though. Or what it would have meant.

She loved what she did. Every late night. Every early morning. The nervous tension. She lived for it, and for Claibourne & Farraday. And this man was trying to take all that away from her. And she'd been about to let him kiss her? No…she'd really, really wanted him to kiss her. This man was special. He exuded power and that scared her just a little bit. But in a way that was hot, and sexy, and…

'Just drop me off at the corner,' Romana said abruptly, as they inched through the early-afternoon traffic. 'You can cut through and avoid the worst of the traffic.' Then, when he didn't answer, 'The auction starts at four, if you can face it, although I'm quite happy to

147

give you time off for good behaviour after this morning.' Her smile felt brittle and false. 'I won't tell if you don't.'

'You're too kind, but really—' he smiled, too, but with the look of a man who wasn't about to fall for such an obvious ruse '—I wouldn't miss it for the world.'

'You must be crazy. Or did you read in this morning's papers that we're auctioning a pair of rhinestone-studded jeans worn by—' she lowered her voice to a suitably awed whisper to murmur the name of a well-known sex bomb '—in her last movie? And that she's going to be there to model them?'

'Incredible as it may seem,' he replied confidentially, 'that story never made it to the *Financial Times*.'

'No? Well, I am surprised. There's big money being spent on pop and sports ephemera.' She shrugged. 'Not to worry. When the jeans make a fabulous amount of money they'll have to report that.'

'Fabulous amounts of money will do it every time,' he agreed. 'I wish you luck.'

'Luck has nothing to do with it. It takes grovelling, begging and pleading on an epic scale to get the kind of stuff that will generate serious publicity. And a lot of personal contacts.'

'I'll bear that in mind should I ever be tempted to get personally involved in such nonsense.'

'You have to get personally involved, Niall. That's the whole point. These people give generously—not just their possessions, but their time—because they know me.' She glanced at her watch. 'As I said, the auction starts at four o'clock, but I suggest you get there early if you want a seat. I'll leave a pass for you at the staff underground car park.'

'No need for that,' he said, turning down the narrow street that led to the rear of the store. 'I brought a change of clothes with me. I just need the use of the chairman's washroom.'

'I'm sorry, Niall, I wish I could help, but India keeps the key chained to her wrist.' Then, prompted by a wicked impulse to annoy him further, she added, 'I'm afraid you're just going to have to stand in line and use mine.'

It was perhaps fortunate that at that moment his attention was claimed by the parking attendant, who was attempting to redirect him to a public car park. She leaned across him to look up at the man. 'It's all right, Greg, Mr Macaulay is working with me on a temporary basis. I'll organise a swipe card for him.'

'Sorry, Miss Claibourne, I didn't recognise you with the headscarf.' He nodded. 'Mr Macaulay.' The barrier was lifted and they drove through.

'Over to the left. You can't use the chairman's washroom, but my father's parking space isn't being used at the moment. You might as well take it while you're shadowing me.'

'Only on a temporary basis, then?'

'Of course.' She smiled. 'Let's face it, if the Farradays should ever manage to regain control of the store, your cousin Jordan is going to want it all for himself.'

'*When,*' Niall said. 'When we take control.' As he took a suit bag from the rear he looked up, briefly, at the imposing building. 'And he's welcome to the parking space. I'll be running the financial aspects of the business from my own offices in the City.' As if on cue his phone rang, and Romana walked ahead while he dealt with some complex detail that needed the personal attention of the boss.

She nodded to the security guard at the rear entrance and headed for the staff lifts, where she waited while he paced back and forth, explaining something at length. Clearly it was rather more than a detail. It made her wonder again why the Farradays had agreed to India's shadowing plan when it must be a major inconvenience. Hadn't they realised what running a vast retail outlet involved? There was a lot more to it than estimating knicker sales.

'You've got it all worked out, then?' she asked, when he finally joined her.

'What? Oh, yes.'

Stupid question. They'd obviously been planning this for months. Years, probably.

'Will you ever bother to come to the store?' she asked.

'Store?' She realised his mind was still on his phone call. 'Oh, probably not,' he said, returning to Claibourne & Farraday business. 'I've got more important things to do than ''shop'' for amusement these days.'

'It's just as well you're in a minority, or we'd all be out of business,' she said. But as she punched in the code to summon the private lift that would take them straight to the top floor she wished it were Niall Macaulay's nose.

She'd thought he'd begun to understand— as he'd spent time with those great kids—to realise that the store was more than just a business. That it had a heart and soul. That it wasn't just a money bin but a real community of staff and customers.

She'd clearly been fooling herself.

Like the kiss that had never happened, it was just self-delusion. Maybe it was time to get real.

As she stepped into the lift she turned to him, holding the door open but blocking his way so that he couldn't join her. 'So tell me, shadow-man, what was the point of your grand tour yesterday? Were you checking for dust behind the fixtures?'

'I thought about it, but since I didn't want to get thrown out I resisted the temptation to run my finger along the skirting boards.'

He did that every time. Made her mad and then made her want to laugh. Or cry. But this time she refused to let herself to be distracted.

'What about sloppy sales staff?' she enquired. 'I'm sure you hoped to find a few of those.' When he didn't answer she put her hand behind her ear. 'Sorry, I didn't catch that.'

'I'm sure every member of your sales staff is a wonderful human being with nothing but the interests of the store at heart,' he assured her, and a smile was a definite possibility. It was in his eyes—just hadn't quite made it to his mouth yet. 'I was simply trying to get a feel for the place.'

'You failed.'

'I didn't realise it was a test.'

'No?' She managed a smile of her own. 'It's a one-way thing, is it? You scrutinise us, but we have to believe you can run a department store simply because you say you can?' She didn't allow him to answer. She knew what his answer would be. That this wasn't about running a store, but about controlling a multimillion-pound business. 'Well, Niall, since you've got half an hour to spare, while I take a shower, I suggest you try again. Only this time look at the people. The customers. The staff. Watch their faces. Listen to the enthusiasm in their voices. And when you've got a handle on the romance of the place, the human factor that makes Claibourne & Farraday great, ask one of the sales staff to ring through to my office and someone will bring you up to the top floor.' She paused. 'But if the magic eludes you, I'd advise you to go back to your counting house...' She indicated the telephone in his hand. 'They need you more than we do. You can safely leave real life to the experts.'

'Real life—'

'Real life,' she repeated, and on a sudden impulse she leaned forward, brushing her lips against his in the merest suggestion of a kiss, dealing with that suggestion of unfinished business in the car park. Just to remind him what real life was all about. Just to remind herself. The heat of his mouth took her by surprise, and for a minute she nearly lost it. 'Oh,' she said, dragging her mind, and her panting hormones, back to business, 'you might find time to work on your apology while you're about it. Since you still have that hurdle to leap.' Then, her finger poised on the door's 'close' button, she smiled at him. 'But just in case I don't see you again, thanks for lunch,' she said, adding before the door shut between them, 'It was really special.'

As the lift began to ascend, Romana slumped against the rear and stared up at the ceiling. She wasn't sure what had just happened. Where that little speech had come from. Or why she was suddenly so very angry with him.

She did know that until the Farradays stopped seeing the store as nothing more than a trophy, to be won at all costs, they were all just going through the motions. That what they were doing was a complete waste of time. It came as something of a shock to realise just how much she hoped she wasn't wasting her time. And not because she was desperate to save the store from being taken over by the 'bean counters'.

She really wanted Niall to see what she saw. To feel what she felt. Not because it was likely to make a difference to the outcome of the dispute. But simply because she suspected that it had been a long time since he'd felt anything very much at all.

Niall remained where he was for a moment, taking a few moments to gather his thoughts, recover from the temptation of a kiss that had seemed to make promises he'd forgotten ever existed. To remind him of the person he once was. Demonstrate just how far his viewpoint had shifted in twenty-four hours. Towards that of Romana Claibourne.

He'd allowed his mind to wander today, forgotten why he was tagging along at the heels of a candyfloss blonde. Distracted by her long legs, the transparently wet cloth clinging to her breasts and the soft warmth of her sugar-pink mouth.

He needed to remember that she'd got wet wrestling with the plumbing—getting on with it instead of shouting for the nearest man. He'd seen for himself that she was a dedicated, hard-working professional. But his mind was stubbornly refusing to move on from his first impression of her. It had bought the illusion—one he suspected she'd gone out of her way to foster—and as a result he hadn't been taking her seriously enough.

The candyfloss blonde, meanwhile, had remained focused on her goal and never once taken her eye off the ball. Well, maybe just once. In the warmth of his kitchen, the comfort of his saggy old sofa, when she'd kicked off her high heels and curled up with her hand beneath her cheek. She'd slept like a baby. Innocent, defenceless.

Louise used to do that.

She'd work on the house all day. He'd walk over from the City at the end of his day and find her there. He'd wake her and they'd make love and then make plans for the rest of their life while they had a late supper. He'd had nearly a year of that…

He'd anticipated spending the rest of life doing that.

That was the only reason it had been in his head when he'd woken Romana, why taking her to bed had seemed such a great idea. The memories. It wasn't personal. It couldn't be personal. Yet just remembering the moment was enough to stir confused guilt-engendering longings, and he raised the back of his hand to his mouth in an attempt to cool it.

He'd come within a heartbeat of kissing her. She'd sat beside him in the car, looked at him with her lips softly parted, waiting for him to kiss her.

With the heat of her lips still on his, he found himself wishing he had.

A woman wearing the burgundy and gold uniform of a store employee paused on her way out. 'That's a private lift. It's just for the offices,' she said helpfully. 'You'll find the store lifts around the corner.'

He nodded his thanks and dragged his mind back into line. Romana was not Louise. Nothing like her. Never would be. And this wasn't a social event; something she seemed to have little difficulty in remembering. Unlike him. But then she had a lot to lose, which tended to concentrate the mind.

Under normal circumstances the enormity of the prize would have kept his own mind fully focused. But this wasn't normal by any standards. It certainly wasn't the way he was accustomed to doing business. He usually conducted business at a distance.

He'd just have to make good use of his time. No business was perfect; he'd find the weak spots and use it against the Claibourne sisters if it came to a court battle.

He didn't need magic for that. He needed facts. He wasn't interested in romance these days. Only profits. And Romana might sleep like a baby, but she wasn't one. No matter how soft her skin, her hair. She was a smart woman with an agenda. Well, he had an agenda of his own, and he was grateful to her for reminding him of his priorities.

He punched in the code to summon the lift. Romana hadn't thought to cloak it behind her hand and it was second nature to him to notice the smallest details. You just never knew when they'd be useful.

Romana kicked off her loafers, then bent to check them for water damage. They were her favourite pair, but they seemed to have survived their inundation. Unlike her trousers, which would never be the same again. Carrying her shoes, she walked barefoot across the thick carpet to her desk and checked for messages. There were dozens, neatly listed by her secretary in order of urgency.

They were going to have to wait. She took a sharp little black suit from her clothes cupboard and spent a sinful five minutes under a hot shower, blasting away the morning, enjoying the luxury of washing her short hair and blowing it dry in minutes.

Then she made-up carefully—she wouldn't have time to do more than retouch her lipstick before the auction started—and put on her designer suit like a knight donning body armour before a battle.

People reacted to the way you looked. If you looked as if you were in control, most people bought it.

When Niall came up to the office, she wanted to be in total control of herself and her surroundings. No more girly nonsense. No more getting soaked through like some girl in a wet T-shirt competition. She was a professional woman and this was her world. Hers. It wasn't Claibourne versus Farraday any more. It was personal. And Niall Macaulay was going to have to work damned hard to wrest it from her.

As she fastened her watch to her wrist, she noted that his half-hour was almost up. When he rang through from the store—always assuming he hadn't just gone back to his office—she was going to be sitting at her desk, dealing with those messages. She smiled at her reflection. He could sit and watch her. Like a good little shadow. Right?

Wrong.

As she opened the bathroom door she discovered that Niall had beaten her to it. He was back in full banker mode. Chalk-stripe suit, white shirt, perfectly knotted tie, his hair gleaming damply from a very recent shower. And he was using her desk. The only thing he hadn't taken over was her phone. He was using a mobile. But she knew that concession was simply to prevent her checking up on his calls. He was making a statement, too. He was saying, In three months from now, this will all be mine.

He looked up as she froze on the threshold. 'At last. I thought you'd drowned in there,' he said, flipping his phone shut.

She refused to show her anger, although the smile took real effort. 'What's your problem? I obviously wasn't holding you up. Did you pick the lock on India's bathroom, just to prove a point?'

'There was no need. Your sister took pity on me.'

'India?' That seemed unlikely.

'No, the other one. Flora? I met her as I got out of the lift. She was in a hurry but she still took a moment to show me your office. And then, since you were still in the shower, she offered me the use of hers. She's a nice girl,' he said. 'Very open. No hidden agenda.'

Oh, good grief! What on earth had Flora been saying to the man? 'She's not a girl. She's a woman. A very clever one,' Romana responded. 'And none of us have a hidden agenda.' Except you, she thought. She just knew he'd got plans for this place that didn't include expanding the customer base. But she kept her suspicions to herself and said, 'I didn't realise she was in the office today.'

'She just came to pick up some notes that were being typed up by her secretary. She said she doesn't spend a lot of time here.'

Oh, great! 'She doesn't need to. She's not an administrator. She contributes in other ways.' Damn, that sounded so defensive.

'Yet she has an office here. Secretarial help. The use of all the facilities. Her own private bathroom, even.' He made his objections sound so reasonable. Before he went in for the kill. 'How much does office space cost in this part of town? Per square foot?'

She was quite certain that, like a good lawyer cross-examining a witness, Niall Macaulay never asked a question to which he didn't already know the answer. 'Too much. And there's never enough of it. We're always looking for extra selling space.'

'Then maybe you should stop indulging yourself in luxury. You don't need all this,' he said, indicating her spacious office with a sweeping gesture. 'Or personal bathrooms. You could bring the customer accounts section up here and give yourself room downstairs for a whole new department.'

Romana's skin goosed as she went cold all over. The best ideas were the simple ones. But if it was so simple why had none of them thought of it? Okay, there were security considerations, but nothing that couldn't be overcome. For the first time since this business began she wondered if, less emotionally involved, the Farradays might be able to see things more clearly. Or were they just plain smarter?

Not necessarily. 'Correct me if I'm wrong, but isn't this how the Farradays laid out the top floor when they were last in control?'

'That was more than thirty years ago,' he pointed out. 'Times have changed. With space at a premium, I'll be recommending that Jordan close the book department, too.'

'We've cut it back already.'

'That just makes a bad situation worse.'

She swallowed. She'd underestimated him. 'Have you any other suggestions?' she asked.

There was nothing to stop her taking advantage of his smart ideas. She wasn't that stupid.

'Suggestions?' he repeated, and smiled as if he knew just what she was thinking—which he almost certainly did. Knew it before she'd thought it, in all probability. 'I'm just here to watch and learn,' he said. 'You're the experts.'

Oh, very cute.

'I'm glad you realise that,' she said. And, shrugging off any suggestion of concern, she moved towards her desk, picked up the list of calls she had to make. 'When you've finished trying my chair for size, Niall, I have work to do.' Then she frowned as her brain caught up with something he'd said earlier. 'Flora showed you to my office? Why wasn't Molly or my secretary waiting for you?' Her frown deepened. 'And what happened to your walk around the store?'

'I walked around the store yesterday. Once was quite enough, and since it seemed pointless bothering your secretary when all I had to do was use the same code as you to summon the lift, I did that.'

Once again words failed her. It was happening a damn sight too often for comfort.

He got up. 'Thanks for the use of your desk.'

'Checking up to make sure things are running smoothly in your absence?'

'They wouldn't dare do anything else. Your chair, however, is on the small size for me.' His smile was perfunctory. 'Tell me more about this auction.'

'You really don't want to come to the auction, Niall. Go back to your bank and your big chair and make some big fat deal. It'll make you a lot happier than watching people throw away excessive amounts of money on trivia.'

'You keep telling me what I don't want to do.'

'Have I been wrong so far?'

'I thought this morning had some notable highlights.'

She didn't ask him to elaborate. She had a pretty good idea of the highlights he had in mind. Instead she glanced at him, giving his chalk-stripe suit the once over before settling herself in a chair that had never seemed too small to her. And was still warm from his body. 'Well, come if you insist,' she said. 'But in that suit everyone will assume you're a dealer.'

'Without a floppy silk handkerchief in my top pocket? I don't think so.' Deep lines were curving into his cheeks as his smile unexpectedly deepened. When she didn't respond, he said, 'Don't be sore because I'm winning, Romana. You're doing really well, but I've been playing these games a lot longer than you have.'

'This isn't a game, Niall. It's real life.' Then, since reminding him of her recent vivid demonstration of 'real life' hadn't been such a good idea, she picked up her phone and began returning calls. But try as she might she was unable to shake off the goosebumps—a sudden fear that she and her sisters were out of their depth and the clever Farraday men would sweep them out of the boardroom without raising a sweat.

*   *   *

Niall had used Romana's desk simply to annoy her, but discovered it hadn't been such a great experience. He'd seen her laughing, genuinely amused, enjoying herself. The frown didn't come close.

She was bent over her desk, phone clamped to her ear as she searched through her desk for something. Her delicate jaw was more than compensated for by the stubborn set of her chin, he thought, as she tucked a stray curl behind her ear. The softness of her lips was counteracted by the crispness of her voice as she passed on the information sought, made a note and moved on to the next message. Completely focused on what she was doing.

She was very easy to watch, he decided. One minute she was catching at her bottom lip with her teeth. The next smiling and nodding as if the person on the other end of the line could see her. She laughed and frowned easily, was quick to reach a decision and wasted no time.

But he didn't want her to look up and catch him watching her, so he followed her example and made use of the time to shift a couple of meetings to the early morning, so that he could spend more time at the store. Then, because she still hadn't finished, he picked up a copy of the glossy burgundy and gold catalogue for the celebrity auction. It was crazy stuff. A football signed by all the members of a premier club. Handwritten recipes of the famous. Original cartoons. Celebrity clothes.

It must have taken an enormous effort to assemble such a collection. And the kind of contacts most PR firms would die for. But, considering the media coverage it would engender, undoubtedly very worthwhile.

She was right about one thing, he realised. He could never do her job. But then it was unlikely anyone could. She was unique. A highly visible social creature everyone seemed to want to know, and yet she was totally dedicated to the store. She'd be tough to replace.

He'd have encouraged Jordan to ask her to join them, but he knew it was a waste of time even approaching her. Presumably she'd use her talents to start her own company. Or maybe she wouldn't bother. She didn't have to do anything. Yet she still put in long hours, worked unbelievably hard.

Which should be telling him something.

'Anything you're likely to make a bid for?'

He looked up, realised that she had finished her calls and was now watching him with a look just short of exasperation. As if she couldn't quite believe he was still there.

'I doubt it.'

'Oh, no. If you're coming I insist you enter into the spirit of thing. Maybe there's something you could buy for...' She shrugged, as if she couldn't imagine who he might want to buy an extravagant gift for. 'Your mother? You do have a mother?' She sounded doubtful.

'I have the full set,' he said. 'Mother, father, two married sisters and an assortment of nephews and nieces.' He shrugged. 'You're right. I'll try very hard to be extravagant in a good cause.'

'Then let's go. You can bring that catalogue with you.'

'I'm surprised you're not already down there briefing the newsmen.'

'Molly's doing that. I'm the auctioneer.'

'You've done it before?'

'Nothing this big.' She pulled a face, walked through the door he held for her. 'I will be so glad when this week is over.'

'What will you do? Take a week off to recover?'

'You're kidding, right?' She ignored the lift and took the stairs, glancing at him as this time she held the door for him. 'How would you put it in your report to Jordan Farraday?' She pitched her voice into BBC announcer mode. '"Miss Romana Claibourne spent week one co-ordinating a number of charity functions with some success, but then, apparently exhausted by the effort involved, used week two for R&R in the South of France".'

'The South of France?' he repeated, to cover the fact that his brain was freewheeling at the thought of Romana Claibourne lying on a sunbed on the deck of a private yacht—he just knew it would be a private yacht—in a bikini.

'Where else at this time of year?' she asked. What was it about Romana Claibourne? His mind hadn't been his own since she'd flung a cup of coffee over him. He forced himself to concentrate on possible holiday resorts for late spring. He'd taken Louise to one of the Greek islands. Tried to get her interested in diving. The sudden urge to rediscover himself, move on, warred with his guilt. 'I'd want to get to the sun with the minimum of travel,' she insisted.

'What? Oh, then go. I won't tell.'

Romana lifted her brows in undisguised disbelief.

'Honest,' he said.

'And I believe you,' she replied. 'Not.' Then, indicating a door, 'We're here.'

Niall opened the staff door to the main restaurant. The largest open space in the store, it was regularly used for lunch-time fashion shows but it had been cleared for the auction, the chairs set out in rows. Not that he could see many chairs. Most were already taken. There were people standing five deep along the walls and the central aisle was bristling with representatives of the media, with their television cameras and Nikons focused on the celebrities who'd come along for free publicity. And the noise was like a solid wall.

'Good grief.'

She looked up at him, apparently sensing that he'd spoken. She couldn't possibly have heard. And then she stood on tiptoe and put her hand to his ear. With her mouth an inch from his cheek she said, 'It's still not too late to make a run for it, Niall.'

She was so close that he could feel her breath whisper warmly against his cheek. See the tiny lines that bracketed the corners of her mouth, lines that lifted her smile into something special. She wasn't smiling now. Despite her cool demeanour, he realised, she was as nervous as a kitten. This was the bungee-jump all over again. Facing her fear and cracking jokes while she did it. Why would she put herself through that? What was she trying to prove?

Whatever the reason, he wasn't going to make it worse this time. And he reached up, took her hand, held it.

'I'm your shadow, Romana. Where you go, I go.'

And then, because he wanted to let her know that faced with the scrum in the restaurant he was on her side, in her corner, a supporter rather than a critic, he bent to kiss her cheek.

He'd meant it to be the merest whisper of a kiss. A ''barely there'' kiss to offer reassurance. To say Go for it and I'm here with you.

Between the thought and the delivery something went wrong. Or very right. Bypassing her cheek and going straight for her mouth the kiss was the culmination of that rush of desire that had all but overwhelmed him when she'd got into his car—that moment when he'd so nearly kissed her, controlling himself just in time. A consummation of the moment when her lips had brushed his after she'd told him it was time to stop thinking and start feeling.

This was feeling.

Gossamer-light, it was a kiss that asked questions he hadn't been aware of framing. A kiss that offered more of himself than he could ever give. And a kiss that promised her she would be wonderful. It might have lasted a second, or a minute; he couldn't have said. Only that it stopped too soon.

As he straightened he saw that her eyes were wide with surprise. Yes, well, she wasn't the only one. An hour ago he'd been promising himself he'd have Romana Claibourne for breakfast. Somewhere deep in his subconscious, he knew, the promise had translated into breakfast in bed.

'You'll be fine,' he said reassuringly. And he knew it was true. She'd do this and no one but him would ever know that beneath the bright smile she was scared rigid.

But Romana wasn't about to admit to nerves. 'Fine?' she snapped, pulling her hand free. For a startled moment he thought she was going to slap him with it. Maybe the assembled ranks of press photographers made her think twice before making a spectacle of them both. Or maybe he'd just imagined the flash of something hot and reckless that sparked behind those big blue eyes. 'Of course I'll be fine, Niall. We'll all be fine. I don't need a Farraday man to hold my hand and tell me that.'

CHAPTER EIGHT

'NICE going.' Molly grinned as she joined her on the podium. 'Not many men can keep a kiss that light and still make it look like hot sex.'

'Kiss?' Romana repeated, her expression blank, her heart pounding like a kettledrum. 'Oh, you mean, Niall? Just now? That wasn't a *kiss*. It was just his way of saying good luck.'

'It would work for me.'

'Really. And how's your lovely husband these days?'

'Adorable. And in for a treat tonight. I feel inspired.'

'Oh, please!'

While Molly went to claim her seat Romana took a sip of water, fanned her cheeks with her notes.

She'd lied. That kiss had been something else. It was everything that she'd seen in his eyes at the drive-thru when she'd thought, hoped, that he was going to kiss her. It was the fizz of electricity that had shot through her when she'd kissed him. Somehow he'd got under her skin, and even now her lips burned, throbbed, wanting more.

She took another sip of water to cool them. Then she picked up her notes and tapped them against the auctioneer's desk, refusing to look across to where he was leaning, one shoulder against the wall, watching her, ignoring Molly's attempts to catch his eye as she patted the seat she'd saved for him.

She didn't want his reassurance. She refused to think about what she really wanted. It wasn't going to happen because all he wanted was Claibourne's. Her store. Her life.

The adrenalin shot of anger was just what she needed to sharpen her up and, picking up the gavel, she brought it down briskly on the desk. In an instant the room was hers.

Only Molly waved her catalogue, still attempting to catch Niall's attention. Romana leaned on the high auctioneer's desk and looked at him. The entire room followed her example. 'Please do take your seat, Mr Macaulay,' she invited, indicating the space her assistant had kept for him. 'So that we can start.'

She'd told him to leave. He no doubt wished at that moment that he'd taken her advice. But it was too late for that. She knew it and so did he. He acknowledged her with the smallest nod and walked across to the front row.

He was halfway there when she asked, 'Did you have trouble parking?' Her tone was conversational, sympathetic even. He settled in the chair, his expression unreadable. She could read it like a book. It said, *You'll pay for this later.* 'You do know that there's a hundred pound fine for latecomers?' she continued, with reckless disregard for the warning.

'Since when?' he asked. Was he playing along? Or genuinely confused? She really didn't care.

'Since now,' she replied. 'I just made it a rule.' The audience, wired for the occasion, was quick to laugh. She held up the gavel for silence. 'And I'm fining you another fifty pounds for questioning the authority of the auctioneer.'

More laughter, but she had the room. They were all watching her now and it took only the lift of a hand to restore quiet.

'Do you have a problem with that?' she asked. Niall held up his hands in surrender, shaking his head, apparently not prepared to risk further penalties. 'Pity,' she said, and once more the audience erupted as she turned to the clerk. 'Make a note, please. One hundred and fifty pounds, Mr Niall Farraday Macaulay.' She looked back to the audience. 'Don't feel too sorry for him, ladies and gentlemen. Mr Macaulay is one of our shareholders, so he can afford to be generous.' And everyone thought that was hilarious, too.

Niall, sitting on the end of the front row—and now the focus of the press photographers—smiled. It might have convinced the cameras, but it didn't convince her.

She didn't think he objected overmuch to being teased in public. If he did that was tough. But she'd just used a very public stage to remind the world that, under their management, Claibourne & Farraday was a very successful venture.

And that was something else.

With luck, the broadsheets would quote her. And if they printed a photograph of Niall, Jordan Farraday would be thoroughly irritated. It would make up for that cosy picture of the pair of them that had appeared in the papers this morning.

It might make Niall Macaulay think twice before patronising her again, too. And as for kissing her... Well, next time, with any luck, he'd choose his time and place with a bit more care. So that she could take him up on the promise his lips had made.

She jammed the brakes on that line of thought and concentrated on the job in hand. 'Right, then. We all know why we're here today, so if you're quite ready, Mr Macaulay, I won't waste any more time...'

The auction went at a furious pace, lasting just over the hour. Romana flirted with the celebrities who had turned up to add a little lustre to the ephemera they'd donated. An entire team of footballers, a TV weatherman and a couple of actors all got the big smile and a kiss for their contribution—without having to pay a hundred and fifty pounds for the privilege—and the press photographers had a field day.

Niall didn't get more than the briefest glance, and that only when he paid a ridiculous amount of money for a signed football shirt for a soccer-mad godson with a birthday on the horizon. The original of a political cartoon for his father and tickets for a gala at the Royal Ballet for his mother didn't even rate a nod.

But when he went to collect his purchases and pay for them, he discovered that Romana had crossed through the 'fines' and initialled the line. 'It was just a joke,' the clerk assured him. 'You don't have to pay.'

'I know,' he said, in turn crossing through the bold 'RC', writing *stet* in the margin and amending the total before handing over his credit card. 'Now the joke's on Miss Claibourne.'

*   *   *

Romana didn't hang around after the auction. She needed some air, some quiet. More than anything, she needed to be on her own.

She kicked off her shoes and began peeling off her suit before her office door clicked shut behind her. She'd got a few minutes while Niall paid for the things he'd bought at the auction and she intended to make good use of them. She was going for a walk and her shadow wasn't invited.

Her secretary looked up from her PC. 'How did it go?' she called through the open door between their offices.

'It was totally crazy. I can't believe the money people were spending.' Even Niall. No. She didn't want to think about Niall. She sensed trouble coming from that direction. Grabbing a top from the neat stack in her closet, she pulled it over her head. 'Any problems here?'

'Nothing I couldn't handle.'

'Thank heavens for that.' She stepped into a pair of softly pleated grey linen trousers, buttoned the waist and pushed her feet into her loafers. 'I'm going to walk home through the park and put my feet up for ten minutes before this evening. But if anyone asks—' and by 'anyone' she meant Niall Macaulay '—I've gone to the dentist.' Even he wouldn't follow her there, she told herself as she grabbed her bag and headed for the door.

She hadn't had a moment to herself since seven-thirty that morning and she just had to get away for half an hour. She needed to forget about the store. Forget about everything.

She opened her door. Niall was leaning against the wall opposite, arms folded, legs crossed at the ankle. Almost as if he'd anticipated her escape bid.

How on earth had he managed to get through the auction scrum so quickly? Stupid question. She'd told the world he was a shareholder. One imperious look and the clerk would have fallen over herself to be helpful.

No. She'd got that wrong. He'd have smiled at the woman. And one smile would have been all it took.

Not that he was smiling now.

She was beginning to suspect he reserved that cool, unnerving look especially for her.

'Going somewhere without your shadow?' he asked.

About to trot out her pre-planned excuse, she thought better of it. This looked too much like a getaway for him to believe such a cliché. And if she protested, he'd insist on coming along to hold her hand. Which would have actually been rather comforting if she really had been going to the dentist.

But, since she wasn't, it would be wiser to stick to the truth.

'I need some fresh air,' she said, but elicited no response. 'And to walk off those French fries.' All that mayo... 'I'm going to walk home through the park. Put my feet up before tonight...' Her voice was rising and she sounded increasingly desperate with each additional elaboration. She stopped before she made a total idiot of herself. Doing it for effect was one thing. Doing it for real held no appeal. 'Thank you for supporting the auction so generously.'

'It's an expensive way to shop.'

'If you're looking for bargains you should try Petticoat Lane.' He still hadn't moved. 'Do you want something, Niall?'

'I came to collect one of the items I paid for.'

She glanced uncertainly at the glossy carrier bag at his feet. 'You're in the wrong place—'

'Oh, no.' The grace with which he moved disguised the speed, and Romana jumped as his hands hit the wall on either side of her, pinning her in place. 'I kissed you and you made me pay for it, Miss Claibourne. Well, I'm here to make a complaint under the Sale of Goods Act, because there's no way I got what I paid for.'

She shook her head, laughed a little. 'Don't be silly, Niall. I crossed it out—told the clerk it was just—'

'A joke. I know. She told me. I paid anyway.'

A quiver of anticipation shivered through her abdomen. A flush of heat and... And this wasn't her. No way. She snapped her eyes shut before he saw the desire hungrily reflected in them. It was the public nature of his kiss that had got her into this situation in the first place. She didn't want to think about what would happen in private. 'I'll see that you get a re- fund—' she began, making a move to go.

He wasn't finished. 'And deny those under- privileged children the benefit of my money? You were quick to tell the world that I can afford it. So come on, Romana, you're the one who keeps telling me it's all for a good cause. Prove to me that this isn't all just PR hype. Show those little children how much you re- ally care.'

She'd known he wasn't a man to sit back and take a public teasing without exacting some kind of reprisal. That was why she'd been in such a hurry to get out of the store. She'd wanted to give him time to calm down before they met at the fashion show.

But caged by his arms, held ransom to his pride, it suddenly occurred to Romana that if he kissed her—really kissed her—she'd be the winner. She'd have broken down that cool, touch-me-not exterior and won their personal battle. Because this was nothing to do with the store. This was something that had started the moment she'd dropped her coffee-carton and he'd looked at her as if she was a stupid blonde bimbo without two brain cells to rub together.

If he kissed her she would prove that he was no better than any other man; he was just as easily dazzled by a short skirt, the twirl of a finger through a curl, a close-fitting dress that gift-wrapped her figure...

How she would enjoy that. In fact, it occurred to her that having Niall Macaulay at her feet would make her very, very happy indeed.

The trick would be to make sure she wasn't dazzled in return. No problem there. She'd grown up with her father as an example of male fidelity. She was immune to the love bug.

Yet with his mouth just inches from hers, his eyes dark with a desire he steadfastly refused to admit, and yet seemingly could not resist, she felt her lips softening, her eyelids drooping as a sweet languor seeped through her limbs.

She felt warm and boneless. As aroused as if his hands were on her body. As if his lips were on hers. She heard the tiny sound that escaped her, a soft whimper that demanded his lips at her throat.

Was this the way men and women were entrapped, became love's fools? The body overriding the brain? Not her. She knew that the sensation was as fleeting as the giddy rush of champagne. Brief and meaningless. But still she closed her eyes and waited.

And waited.

When she opened them again, she discovered that Niall hadn't moved a muscle. She said nothing, was afraid even to swallow, certain that to draw any kind of attention to herself was to invite disaster. But then, as if dragging himself from some deep pit of concentration, he finally straightened, letting his hands drop to his sides.

'Thank you, Romana,' he said.

For what? She mouthed the words, but the sound remained stuck somewhere, deep in her throat. She cleared her throat and tried again. 'For what?'

'For establishing a point of principle. For admitting that I have a case.' And with that he stepped back, picked up his carrier bag and walked in the direction of the lift.

'That's it?' she demanded of his retreating back. 'You were simply establishing a point of principle? You don't want—' About to say, your pound of flesh, she thought better of it. 'Settlement in full?'

'The kiss will wait,' he replied, turning to face her but continuing to walk backwards, as if he found it necessary to put the maximum distance between them. 'Don't worry. I'll tell you when.' And then he disappeared from her sight as he took the turning to the lift.

Don't worry? Romana remained where she was, pinned to the spot as she re-ran the encounter in her head. *He'd tell her when?* What the heck did that mean? That he'd snap his fingers and say 'when' at some moment of his choice and she'd have to jump? No...he wouldn't snap his fingers. He was a man who'd never had to snap his fingers in his life. One look was all it took.

'Oh, sugar,' she said.

The words were little more than a whisper, a croak.

Niall returned to his office. He should have returned the minute he got that phone call. He'd told himself that Farraday pride was more important. But it wasn't Farraday pride that had kept him at the store that afternoon. It was Romana Claibourne.

And he was just as determined to be at the fashion show tonight. He'd just royally turned the tables on her and he wanted to see her sweat.

From now on, every moment they were in public together she would be on tenterhooks, waiting for him to choose his moment to collect his one-hundred-and-fifty-pound kiss. And regretting every giggle she'd extracted from her audience at his expense.

Not that he cared about that. What had made him angry was that he'd been genuinely concerned that she was pushing herself, over and over, to do things that scared her out of her wits. And that she'd spurned his care as if she thought he was trying to trick her in some way.

He'd thought they'd moved beyond that. He'd hoped they had.

He'd very nearly blown it, though. After her reaction to that earlier kiss he'd expected considerably more resistance, and when she'd looked up at him, her eyes dark, her mouth softly parted over her pretty little teeth, his own reaction had been swift and urgent. He'd gone after her seeking a little payback. What he'd got in return had been very nearly a knockout blow.

He'd come close to being blown away. To taking everything she was offering and then some.

Because no one had come close to kick-starting his heart after the loss of Louise, he'd begun to believe that no one ever could, that he could play mind games with Romana Claibourne and not get hurt. He'd been wrong about that.

Which was why he knew he must never claim his kiss. Because one kiss would never be enough. Because even one kiss would be a total betrayal of a woman who'd died because he'd teased her into doing something she'd feared.

But for now that decision would remain a secret between him and his conscience.

Romana, for once, played down her clothes. Since there was no way she could compete with the models for sheer physical presence and beauty, she decided on total contrast and wore a pair of well-cut black trousers, a black silk shirt and a simple pair of silver ear-studs. She'd be backstage, co-ordinating the running plan, and black would make her easy to find amongst the jewel-bright wedding and honeymoon clothes.

Too easy.

Niall spotted her straight away. His dinner jacket was equally stark against the vivid fabrics as he made his way through the crush towards her, apparently oblivious to the half-naked models who were totally unselfconscious about their bodies. His eyes were only for her.

A tiny flutter of apprehension battered against her midriff, even though common sense assured her that he would pick somewhere far less hectic to claim his kiss. Somewhere that would involve maximum embarrassment. Amongst this noisy crush of air kisses and da—arlings, one more kiss, no matter how passionate, would pass totally unnoticed.

His tie was crooked again, she noticed, and since she didn't want him to think she was avoiding him, that she was afraid, she turned towards him and reached up to straighten it.

'Maybe you should give this up and go for something ready-tied,' she suggested as she twitched it into place. 'I'll get the menswear department to send you some to try.' Only when she was quite satisfied did she allow herself to look up and meet his eyes.

His expression was impossible to read, but it was nothing that she had done or said. He wasn't looking at her. His gaze was riveted on something behind her. 'Niall? Are you okay?' she asked. When he didn't answer, she turned to see what he was looking at. A raven-haired model was being fastened into a classic white bridal gown, laughing at something her 'groom' was saying. For a split-second the scene looked real. Bride. Groom. Happy ever after.

'Look, you can't stay out here. The girls will object,' she said, seizing the first excuse that came into her head. And, turning him away from the scene, she took him by the arm and directed him very firmly towards the door. 'Molly's out there somewhere. She'll look after you, find you a seat.'

'No.' He found a smile from somewhere. Somewhere bleak. 'I believe you were right, Romana. I've had all the ''fun'' I can take for one day. If you'll excuse me from our supper date?'

'Gladly,' she said, feeling oddly bleak herself. 'To be honest I was hoping you'd forgotten.'

That raised the temperature of his smile to wry. 'I'll bet.'

She nodded. 'Look, I have to get back there.' She waved a hand towards the rising hysteria behind her. Then, because she was in danger of spilling a tear, she turned and walked quickly away from him. Damn, damn, damn!

What was it about a man wearing his broken heart on his sleeve that was so... *heartbreaking*?

She should just be glad he was out of her hair for the evening. That he was one less thing to worry about.

But the thought of him going back to that huge empty house with the image of a young bride in his head made her want to weep.

Instead, she blinked hard and set about re-storing order to chaos.

'Romana?' One of the models was looking at her as if expecting some response. 'I said we're all going through to have supper, then on to a club maybe. Do you want to join us?'

'Thanks, but it's been a long day. I think I'll just go home and fall into bed.'

'If it's with the dishy bloke who was in here earlier, I don't blame you.'

She didn't bother to correct the girl, but found her jacket and walked through to the main entrance of the hotel. 'Taxi, Miss Claibourne?'

'Please.'

The commissionaire summoned a black cab, opened the door for her and she climbed in. 'Where to, miss?' the driver asked as he headed up the ramp to the main road.

Where to? She thought about her comfortable flat, the lavender-scented linen on her bed waiting to enfold her, lull her to sleep. And she turned her back on them. 'Take me to Spitalfields.'

The man turned round in his seat. 'Spitalfields, miss?' he repeated, to confirm he'd heard right.

She wasn't sure either, but she had to go anyway. All evening she'd been co-ordinating the fashion show, coping with minor crises,

being the totally efficient Miss Romana
Claibourne, Public Relations Director of
Claibourne & Farraday, her mind apparently
focused on the job.

But on a different level she'd been somewhere else. In a large lonely kitchen with a
man she should be kicking while he was down.
Instead, she'd been haunted by the thought of
Niall alone with his memories.

And she had known she'd never be able to
sleep until she reassured herself that he was all
right.

'This is it, miss.'

She glanced up at the house. The front windows were dark, but a faint glow of light fil-
tered through from somewhere at the back and
she got out. The quiet was illusory, she discovered. From beyond the old market she
could hear the sound of music coming from
the many restaurants that had sprung up in the
area. 'Will you wait, please? I won't be long.'

The driver left the meter running while she
crossed the narrow pavement and walked up
the steps to the front door. She lifted the

knocker and held it for a moment, hesitating between the cast-iron certainty that she was about to make a fool of herself and the knowledge that she could do nothing else. Then she let it fall with a sound that seemed to echo throughout the house.

She waited. Nothing happened.

She glanced at the cab driver. He was talking into his radio while keeping an eye on her, taking care that his expensive fare didn't make a run for it and disappear up some back street. She didn't blame him.

She turned back to the door and lifted the knocker again. Before she could bring it down the door opened, wrenching the thing from her hand so that she nearly overbalanced and fell into the hall.

'What is it?' Niall, still in his dress shirt but with his tie pulled loose, the top button undone, sounded thoroughly irritable. Then, as she recovered her balance and the light from the street fell on her, he said, 'Romana? What on earth are you doing here?'

There were any number of answers to that question.

I was just passing and I thought I'd take you up on your offer of the grand tour...

There's been a change of plans for tomorrow...

I've mislaid my doorkey and I need a bed for the night...

But only the truth would do. 'I was concerned about you, Niall. When you left the Savoy you looked...bleak.'

'You mean you thought you'd find me drowning my sorrows in a bottle of Scotch? That would make excellent ammunition in the war between the Claibournes and the Farradays, wouldn't it? India would undoubtedly award you an A for effort.'

'Are you?' she asked, ignoring his sarcasm. 'Drowning your sorrows?' He was somewhat dishevelled, with what looked like a cobweb caught in his hair, but he didn't look as if he were drowning in Scotch or anything else.

'Oh, hell. Look, you'd better come in,' he said, holding the door wide for her.

'I've got a taxi waiting.'

He glanced at the black cab, waiting at the kerb. 'Let it go. I'll take you home.' He instantly picked up on her doubtful look. 'Don't worry, I haven't found a problem yet that looked better through the bottom of a bottle.' And he crossed to the cab, glanced at the meter and offered the driver a banknote.

The driver took it, but he didn't move. 'Is that all right with you, miss?'

Niall turned to her but said nothing, leaving the decision to her. What decision? She was there, wasn't she? Of course she was going to stay. 'Yes, thank you. I'll be fine,' she said, reassuring the man.

'You're sure?'

'Quite sure.' The man made a move to get change, but Niall waved it away.

'Come on through,' he said as, with his arm at her back, he ushered her inside. 'I'm in the kitchen.' He shrugged. 'I'm always in the kitchen. The rest of the house is somewhat…unfinished.'

'Show me,' she said. 'I want to see it all.'

CHAPTER NINE

NIALL looked down at her uncertainly. 'Now?' he said.

'Why not? You promised me the grand tour.' She shrugged and added, 'Unless you've got something better to do? Or if the bottle is a more attractive proposition?' He deserved that, she told herself, for suggesting her sole motive in checking up on him was to discover if he was in the habit of drowning his sorrows. It spoke volumes for the man that she hadn't even considered it. 'I can always ring for a minicab.'

After a moment he shrugged, then turned and flicked on a switch, flooding the hall and stairs with light. She began to unfasten her jacket, but he stopped her. 'You might want to hang onto that. The heating system on the upper floors is a bit basic. The kind that involves newspaper, kindling and coal.' He stood back, offering her the stairs. 'We'll start at the top.'

The house was on four floors. The top floor consisted of a series of small attic rooms in which the possessions accumulated over many years were stored, no longer needed, but too full of precious memories to be thrown away.

In one of them there was a woman's bicycle. One of those old-fashioned sit-up-and-beg jobs with a basket in front and a big chrome bell. Perfect for whizzing through City traffic. 'I have one of these,' she said, wiping her finger along the handlebars. 'I used it when I was at college.'

'These days you prefer taxis?'

'Not always.'

Niall closed the door without comment and led the way down to the next floor. 'This was Louise's office,' he said, opening the door to a room that overlooked the rear of the house. The dust lay thick and white over everything, as if nothing had been disturbed since she'd died. Romana, on the point of recommending a good cleaning firm, for once held her tongue.

When he was ready to let go he was quite capable of checking out the *Yellow Pages* himself. 'There's nothing much to look at up here, unless you're thrilled by eighteenth-century building techniques,' he said, after a moment. He took her silence for a negative. 'This was domestic territory. Children and servants. In those days they saved the really expensive stuff for the public rooms.'

'You said you'd uncovered some of the original decoration?'

'In the drawing room.'

'Show me.'

They descended to the next floor where Niall opened a pair of panelled doors and switched on an overhead light. Romana wasn't sure what she'd expected to find, but the dreary faded paint and barely visible floral decorations left her distinctly underwhelmed.

'Louise researched the history of the house and discovered that this room was painted in 1783 on the occasion of the marriage of the silk merchant who owned it to his second wife. It would have been the very best that money could buy.' He ran his hand over the walls. 'The floral frieze was hand-painted by a local artist who produced designs for the silk weavers.'

'Really? And it was all so expensive that no one has been able to afford to redo it since?'

'Louise thought she'd just repair the damage in the corner and keep it the way it is,' he said, missing the sarcasm. Or maybe just ignoring it.

She looked around. The drawing room was beautifully proportioned, with high ceilings and three long sash-cord windows that looked out over the street, a floor below them. Maybe she was a phillistine, but she thought what the walls needed was a couple of coats of good emulsion in a cheerful colour, with the doors and windows picked out in white.

'Is it all like this?'

He made a 'help yourself' gesture, standing back while she toured the landing, opening the doors, glancing in at the rooms opening off the main landing. The only room that was truly habitable was the master bedroom. Even a man so lost in love he would put up with this mess would expect somewhere comfortable to sleep. And a well-fitted bathroom.

Not that she noticed the decoration particularly. The only thing that caught her eye was the silver frame containing the portrait of a lovely young woman with glossy raven hair, dark sparkling eyes. She could see why the sight of the model at the fashion show had drained the colour from his face, driven him home. The likeness was superficial, but in a wedding dress, wearing a veil…

'What do you think?' he said, from the doorway.

She closed the bedroom door behind her. 'You don't want to know what I think,' she said, shivering a little. And not just with the cold.

'Come on, Romana, don't be shy. It doesn't suit you.'

'It's foot in the mouth time again, is it? Time to tell you what your best friends are too kind to say?' He didn't answer, knowing full well that she was simply playing for time and hoping he'd let her off the hook. But why would he? Her stuck on a hook, out of his way, would suit him very nicely. 'Very well,' she said, when she could delay no longer, 'I think you should move.'

'What?'

Well, that had certainly got his attention. 'Historically I'm sure all this is totally fascinating. A restoration project might even make good television. But only a historian would consider living with the result.'

'But Louise was—'

'I know. She was an architectural historian. But you're not. You're a man of your time. You understand that when your silk merchant decorated this room in 1783 he was showing off. Big time. Using the latest style, the most expensive decorative techniques to tell the world that he was a man of substance. If Louise had learned anything from her history books she'd have encouraged you to do the same. Life moves on, Niall. You can't live in a museum.'

'That's your considered opinion, is it? Get in a firm of decorators and leave them to it?'

'No.' Oh, she could see the possibilities. It was a house made for a big family, to be lived in from attic to basement. A wonderful home. But even with the dust swept away and the walls repainted it wouldn't be the home for a brooding widower who was stuck in a rut that was getting deeper with every passing year. 'My considered opinion is that you should buy yourself a light, airy loft-apartment overlooking the river and move on.' His expression suggested she didn't know what she was talking about. He was wrong. 'You bought this house for Louise because you loved her and because it was in your power to make her dream come true. But you were way off track when you said she'd give you hell for not finishing what she'd started.'

'Is that it?' His jaw tightened as he held back the things he wanted to say to her. Mostly, Romana suspected, along the lines that she didn't have a clue what she was talking about. 'Have you quite finished?'

'No, I haven't.' Not by a country mile. 'You're a businessman, Niall, not a historian. What Louise would give you hell for is staying here and ignoring your own natural instincts to capitalise on your assets. This is an upwardly mobile area—you'd make a good return on your investment.'

'Well, thanks for reminding me that I'm a banker, with a profit margin where my heart should be—'

But nothing was going to stop her now. 'You said it,' she reminded him. Then, 'What is worse, Niall, what would make Louise really unhappy, is that you're doing *nothing*. You're not living in this house; you're not restoring it. You're just letting it grow cold around you while you grieve.' Then she drew in a shaky breath. 'Now I'm finished.' And she moved her shoulders in what might have been a shrug. 'You did ask.'

'So I did.'

'And?'

'And I think now might be a good time to try that drink.'

Romana followed Niall into the kitchen. There were papers and envelopes scattered over the table, and he quickly swept them up into a box which he dumped on the floor by the dresser. She put a lid on her curiosity and crossed to the sink, where she filled the kettle.

'What are you doing?' he asked.

'Making a drink. That's what you wanted. Tea or coffee?' she enquired. 'Since you've offered to drive me home.'

'I said I'd take you home, not that I'd drive you.' And he took a bottle of brandy and a couple of glasses from the dresser. 'So, now you've dissected my character and put my life to rights, why don't you take your coat off, draw up a chair and tell me what makes Romana Claibourne run. Why she does things that scare her rigid. Why she's not tucked up in bed right now with some man who adores her.'

He'd bared his soul to her and now it was her turn? She responded by opening the fridge door. 'Have you eaten?' she asked.

'Isn't that my line?'

'Not exclusively. And I'd rather have a glass of wine than brandy. If there's a choice. If not, I'll stick with tea.' She checked the sell-by date on a box of eggs that had been bought in the food hall at C&F. 'At least you're not above shopping for food,' she remarked, adding a block of cheese and a bag of ready-washed salad to her food cache and putting them on the kitchen table.

'I have a standing order delivered weekly.'

Romana slipped off her jacket and hung it over a chair. 'You have your groceries delivered?'

'I work long hours,' he said, returning the brandy to the dresser and opened the door to a pantry lined with wine racks. 'Especially when I'm running a bank and shadowing you. Red or white?'

'White, please.' Romana worked her way around the kitchen, opening cupboard doors until she found a basin and an omelette pan, while he peeled the foil from the neck of the bottle. 'Have you got a grater?' she asked.

'Probably.'

When he didn't elaborate, she said, 'Can you give me a clue as to its likely whereabouts? And I could do with a whisk.'

'I've no idea where the grater is, but the whisk is in the toolshed. I used it to stir some paint.'

'Paint?' She raised her eyebrows. *'Paint?'* she repeated. 'When?'

'Not recently,' he admitted, pulling the cork. 'But you don't need a whisk to make an omelette. A fork will do the job more than adequately. You'll find one in that drawer over there.'

About to tell him what he could do with his fork and his omelette, she belatedly caught the glint of challenge in his grey eyes. Wind her up and watch her go. Her sisters had used to do that all the time, until she'd realised it was no fun for them if she didn't erupt on cue. But something about Niall Macaulay had got beneath her carefully established guard.

'Thank you,' she said, refusing to perform.

'Tell me,' he continued, pouring the wine as she cracked the eggs with more force than was absolutely necessary, 'what is it like to be the youngest of three, each with a different mother? How did you get on as children?'

'Digging for dirt, Niall?' she asked, as she picked shell out of the egg before fetching a fork and finally locating the grater in a drawer. 'Hoping to set us against one another? It won't work.'

'No. I can see that you're quite a team.'

'You mean Jordan has already dug as deep as he knows how and has figured that out for himself.'

'Peter Claibourne's marriages are scarcely a secret. They made all the gossip columns at the time. I was just interested in the reality. I mean one of you being abandoned by your mother might have been bad luck, but all three of you...'

He was attempting to turn all the loose emotion flying about back on her, she realised. Distract her from his tragedy. But this was an old story.

'Holding onto his wives may not have been a strong point, but my father made a virtue of keeping his children.' He'd had the money and the lawyers to ensure he did. 'Fortunately none of our mothers remained Mrs Claibourne for long enough for us to notice them, and since we all lived together in a well-run nursery with a succession of totally efficient nannies...'

She shrugged. She'd been shrugging all her life, pretending it didn't hurt that her mother hadn't been strong enough to take her with her when she left. It didn't hurt that the pay-off for leaving her behind, no matter how big, had been compensation enough for losing her daughter. But then her mother hadn't wasted time in restocking her nursery; Romana had seen the 'happy families' pictures of her with her four beautiful children in magazines that made a virtue of such stuff.

But she'd never let anyone see her pain.

'Your father didn't have much luck with his wives.'

'He went for looks over substance every time,' she agreed, resolutely refusing to let him get beneath her skin. 'And you have to work at relationships. Not one of my father's strong points.' Not even with his children, despite his determination to keep them. And then, because she'd said more than she'd intended, she shrugged again. 'Flora moved in with her mother when she was sixteen,' she said—as if that somehow countered his criticism. 'India's mother is something of mystery, though. She went back to the ashram where they'd met on the hippie trail. She wasn't the mercenary type, you see, but a genuine flower-child, while my father couldn't wait to throw off the beads and revert to the Savile Row three-piece suit.' She couldn't resist a little dig at Niall's own preferred form of attire.

'Maybe he didn't have much choice. Your grandmother was a formidable woman by all accounts.' Then, 'I think that's probably enough cheese, Romana. Unless your plan is to lay me low with a high-cholesterol, high-fat heart-stopper?'

She looked at the heap of cheese. 'Oh, good grief. I've grated it all. Never mind, you can use it to make sandwiches…or something.'

'Here...' He passed her a glass of wine. 'You sit and drink that slowly. I'll cook.' He took a bottle of olive oil from a cupboard and shook some into the pan, turning up the heat. Then he stirred up the eggs with an easy competence that suggested it wasn't the first time he'd done it.

Romana leaned back against the table and watched him work, his sleeves rolled back over powerful forearms, the overhead light picking out the cobweb that still clung to his dishevelled hair.

'What were you doing when I arrived?' she asked, ignoring his invitation to sit but instead leaning back against the table and watching him as she sipped the wine.

He glanced at her. 'Doing?'

'You looked as if you'd been—'

'Drinking? That's what you said.'

'No, that's what you said.' She shook her head. 'You looked...still look...as if you'd been digging around in the cupboard under the stairs. A bit dusty, a bit ruffled.' She reached up and picked the cobweb out of his hair, holding it out for him to see. He glanced at the cobweb, then at her, and suddenly she realised how close they were. Close enough for her to see what she had been trying so desperately hard to ignore.

Not an enemy who was going to do his level best to take her world away, but the kind of man for whom the world would be well lost.

'Did you find what you were looking for?' she asked, desperate to break the bond of tension that held them locked, inches apart, unable to advance or retreat.

'Who said I was looking for anything?' he asked, and looked away. She stepped back as he poured the egg into the pan. It sizzled fiercely as, still using only the fork, he pushed it towards the centre. Then he added a handful of cheese, totally absorbed in his task.

Romana glanced across at the box by the dresser. Papers and envelopes. One large envelope bearing the name of a society photographer.

He turned when she didn't answer and, following her gaze, said, 'I needed...' For a moment he seemed to struggle for breath. 'I needed to find the photographs. After tonight. That girl in the wedding dress was so like her—'

He didn't have to explain which photographs. 'You think so? There's a photograph of Louise in your bedroom, and apart from her colouring I didn't see much likeness to the model.' She picked up the box and put it on the table, then the envelope. 'But let's have a look,' she said, matter-of-factly.

'No!' He reached out, grasped her wrist to stop her sliding out the carton of proofs. 'I don't think now is the time.'

She indicated the hob. 'Is something burning?'

He turned and grabbed the pan, rescuing the omelette before it was ruined. He flipped it over, broke it in two and divided it between two plates. 'It's a bit brown on the outside,' he said, turning as she slipped the proofs from the carton so that they slid across the table, a jumble of bright images.

He snapped back as if punched.

She took one of the plates from him. 'Fork?' she prompted. For a moment she thought he was going to snatch the plate back and throw her out. But he was still in control. Still keeping it all buttoned up. The pain, the heartbreak. Not letting anything show in his face. Very determinedly not looking at the photographs, he turned, took a couple of forks from the drawer and handed one to her.

No wonder his eyes appeared stone-cold. When you were hanging onto control by your fingernails, refusing to confront the pain, you couldn't risk any kind of emotional response.

He leaned back against one of the units, taking a mouthful of egg and melted cheese, making himself go through the motions, acting as if nothing was wrong. But she knew now that it was all a sham. She'd had a glimpse of something else, something warm and alive, a heart still beating behind the brick wall he'd built around it.

She took courage from the fact that he was staying as far away from the photographs as he could without being too obvious about it.

She was getting to him. Maybe, if she pushed it, she could blow that control apart and give him back his humanity.

Romana ignored the photographs. Instead, she put down her plate and riffled through the contents of the box. It made her feel like a voyeur, picking over the entrails of someone else's life, but she was determined to goad some spark of reaction from him.

The box was full of letters, mementoes, the kind of snapshots that all people in love take of each other. Silly stuff. Stuff no one else should ever see. Unable to go through with it, she turned away, took another mouthful of the omelette. Like him, she was going through the motions. Acting as if everything was perfectly normal.

'My sisters came round and cleared the house before I got home. Took away her clothes, the wedding presents. Put all that stuff in a box to be dealt with later,' he said at last, cracking. 'When I could face it.'

'You shouldn't have left it so long.'

'Is there a time scale for these things?' he asked. 'I didn't know.'

'You can't bury grief. You have to deal with it.' While he refused to confront the pain he would remain locked in this empty house, unable ever to move on. 'Talking about people we've loved and lost keeps them alive. You need to look at the pictures, remember the day, the things she said, you said—'

'Stop it!' For a moment his eyes flashed, hot and quick. 'You don't know what you're talking about!' Then he made a hopeless little gesture with his hand. 'I hope to God that you never find out…'

He clung to the plate as if it would protect him. But he wasn't eating. She took it from him. Took his hand. 'At least you had someone who loved you above everything. You know how that feels. You will always have that.' While she had never had anyone who cared for her first, last, always.

He was right. She couldn't feel his pain. But she was feeling something that hurt. Something that twisted like a knife in her gut at the sight of him locked in grief for his dead wife. It was why she was here, in his kitchen, instead of tucked up in her lonely bed, taking care not to ever get emotionally involved.

But if she did nothing else good in her life she would help him confront his demons. And, with every appearance of carelessness, she picked up an eight-by-ten glossy of Louise arriving at the church. 'The model reminded you of your wedding day?' she asked.

'You have to ask? You told me to stay away.'

'Yes…' She looked at the photograph of Louise, laughing as the wind snatched at her veil. Glowing with joy. Full of life. She'd tried to protect him and she'd hustled him out of the dressing room. 'I was wrong, though. You were wrong. The fashion show had nothing to do with this. That was just make-believe, a dream image of the perfect bride. Louise was a real woman, not some fanciful illusion of perfection stage-managed to sell a dream. Look at her, Niall.' She held out the photograph so that he could see it, but he kept his gaze fixed rigidly on her face. 'You loved her with all your heart. And she loved you. You'll always have that. These are just paper memories.' She reached out to him, took his hand, put the photograph into it. 'Look at her now and remember what you had, not what you've lost.'

He didn't look down. 'I can't…'

'Look at her! You loved her. You can't shut her away in a cupboard at the back of your heart.'

'A cupboard at the back of my heart?'

Oh, no. She wasn't going to allow him to mock her. To laugh at her clumsy analogy and sweep the photographs away. 'You have got a heart?' she demanded.

After an endless pause, in which the only sound was the ticking of an old wall-mounted pendulum clock, he let his gaze drop from her face to the photograph he was holding. He looked at it for a long time. For a long time his face showed nothing. Then he reached out for the pictures scattered across the table. Scooping up a handful, and gripping her hand tightly in his, he walked across to the sofa and sat down, leaving her with no option but to join him. Only when she'd flopped beside him, and the uncertain springing had thrown them together, did he release her and begin to go through the pictures one by one in grim silence.

There were more of Louise arriving at the church with her father. Niall and Jordan in grey morning coats. Niall looked unbelievably younger. Far more than four years could account for. Or maybe it was simply that he was no longer so carefree, so utterly happy.

'Jordan was your best man?' she asked.

He nodded.

There was a blush of little bridesmaids in white and peach dresses. A couple who had to be Niall's parents, with two pretty young women. 'These are your sisters?' She prodded and prompted, forcing him to respond.

'Cara and Josie,' he confirmed. 'It was Josie's boy that I bought the football shirt for. He's eight next month.'

And, as if that had somehow released the floodgates, he began to talk, pointing out the important players, family, friends, all celebrating this happiest of days. There was one of Bram and his young brothers. 'They did this,' Niall said, showing her a photograph of their departure from the hotel. The open car, a vintage Rolls, was decorated with balloons and old shoes, an ''L'' plate and ''Just Married'' were tied to the rear bumper. Louise and Niall were looking back at the camera, waving and laughing.

A tear hit the photograph. For a moment Romana thought it was hers. But then Niall turned to her and she saw that he, too, had tears streaming down his cheeks. There was nothing more she could say. All she could do, as the photographs slithered to the floor, was open her arms and hold him while he let out the pent-up grief of four long years.

CHAPTER TEN

'IT'S ALL right, Niall. Just let it out...' The words she murmured didn't matter. She just wanted him to know that she understood the bottled-up grief—that desperate feeling of being left behind, abandoned.

She kissed his forehead, then his temple, murmuring her own heartbreak as she comforted him, telling him things that had been locked up inside her for as long as she could remember. And all the time she held him, his head at her breast, the fingers of one hand tangling in his hair, the other cradling his cheek.

'You're not alone,' she whispered as she kissed the tears from his eyes, kissed the line of his jaw, her hand slipping to his neck as he turned and she nuzzled tenderly at his throat. 'I'm here.'

'Romana...' Her name was wrenched from him, warning her to stop even as his arms tightened about her as if he would never let her go. 'Romana,' he said, as if she was all that was standing between himself and hell.

She murmured his name in echo of hers, closing her eyes and tilting her head back a little to offer him that total surrender which was the true and perfect solace a woman offered to the man she loved when he was in pain. Offering the cradle of her arms, her body, a place where he could forget everything, asking nothing in return.

He lifted his head, looked up, and when he once more whispered her name there was a new intensity to his voice. In the quiet still of the kitchen the mood had altered subtly, and she knew that he was with her, seeing *her*.

'Romana.' He said it again, over and over, as if it was a new word, as if he had never seen her before—as if he'd suddenly opened his eyes and seen a new world. 'Romana...'

'I'm here,' she said. And she slipped the top button of her shirt. And then the second.

He reached up, and for a moment she thought he would stop her, but he just touched her hand briefly before raising his fingers to her face, cradling her cheek. Looking at her. It seemed for ever—as if he were trying to read her deepest thoughts.

Whatever he saw in her eyes must have been what he was hoping to see, and he captured her face between his hands, leaning into a kiss that was at once assured yet sweetly hesitant, his lips silently seeking her consent every step of the way.

Is this good for you? he seemed to be asking her. Do you like this?

Her answer, with her lips, her tongue, her hands, was yes...and yes...and yes... And as his mouth grew more demanding her own need matched his hunger and she slipped back against the cushions.

'I want to touch you,' he said. 'I want to undress you...'

In answer she reached up and began to unfasten his shirt studs. There was a pause that seemed to last a year before he reached out to touch her throat with the back of his fingers, stroking them down the length of her breastbone until his hand reached the soft curve of her breasts.

Again he waited for her, silently asking the question. Do you want this? In reply, she unfastened the front of her the black lace bra.

'Silk,' he whispered as he opened his hand to encompass her breast. 'Pure silk.' And then he pushed her back into the soft cushions, going down with her to take his mouth on the same exploring journey as his hand.

Every touch, every kiss, every murmur was slow and sure. The brush of his lips, the melting heat of his eyes, the intimate pressure of his body bombarding her with sensations that aroused her to an almost painful awareness of her desire for him, her longing for this.

The touch of his skin beneath her hands, the roughness of hair over his chest, his unmistakable arousal—all was exciting and new, and Romana held her breath, afraid that anything she might say or do would break the spell. Then she whimpered softly as he eased away, and this time when he murmured her name that was a question too.

'Romana…?'

In answer she reached up and put her arms around his neck, bringing him back to her. 'I want to touch you,' she said, repeating his own words back to him. 'I want to undress you.'

And slowly, tenderly, they each had their wish, learning each other's desires, pleasures, until the heat built between them and they lost any sense of place or time.

It would have been quite perfect if, as he came, the name on his lips had been hers.

For a moment he was utterly still. Louise's name had shocked them both out of the sweet aftermath of love. Neither of them breathed. The silence so dense it vibrated against her eardrums.

'Romana,' he said. Too late. 'You know I didn't… I wasn't thinking…'

Niall didn't know what he was thinking. He'd held Romana in his arms, had made love to her with a passion that he'd thought beyond him. She was the woman he wanted. Still wanted. No one else.

And yet Louise had been there with them. They had been talking about her. Remembering her. Her photographs were scattered about the floor where they'd fallen. She was there with them, waiting for him to say goodbye.

'It's all right, Niall. I understand.'

'Do you? I don't.' All he understood was that he'd hurt her in a way that he didn't know how to mend. That it certainly wasn't all right. It was as wrong as it could be. But as he reached out in an attempt to hold her, reassure her, she turned from him, swinging her legs to the floor, gathering her clothes from where they'd fallen amongst the wedding photographs.

Shutting him out.

'You needed someone, Niall,' she said, matter-of-factly. 'I was here. Don't let's make a drama out of it. Would you call me a taxi while I use the bathroom?'

'I'll take you.' He wasn't asking her, he was telling her. He couldn't let her just walk away, shrug off something that for him had been a revelation. For a moment he thought she would argue, insist on a taxi. But perhaps she'd decided it would be easier than facing the awkward silence as they waited for it to arrive because she finally nodded.

Romana was dying inside. As Niall bent to pick up his shirt from among the scattered photographs she thought she'd never seen a man look so pale. He was pinched white about the nose, and she thought her heart would break at bringing him to such a pitch of guilt.

Guilt about betraying the precious memory of his wife. And now the additional guilt about what he'd done to her.

She'd thought she could solve all his problems, but she'd only made things worse. Clutching her clothes to her, she stooped to help him pick up the photographs.

'Leave them,' he said, catching her hand. They stared at one another, and for a moment Romana thought he was going to put his arms about her, hold her. 'I'll get them later.'

He stood up and she took the chance to escape up the stairs to the only bathroom she'd seen.

When she emerged he was standing in the bedroom, wearing jeans and a soft sweater, car keys in his hand. 'You don't have to do this,' she said. 'You've had a drink...'

'I haven't had more than a mouthful of wine.' He paused. 'My hospitality is well-intentioned, but somehow it never quite lives up to the promise.'

She thought he was talking about rather more than food and wine.

'Don't underrate yourself.' He looked pale in the soft lighting. 'You make a mean ome-lette.' And she made herself smile. Things were bad enough without throwing a wobbly because he was still in love with his wife. She could at least spare him that.

She'd been the one who'd wanted to give without any thought of self. Or so she'd be-lieved. Self-delusion was a dangerous thing. And they still had nearly a month of shadow-ing to get through.

'Will I see you tomorrow? At the store?' she asked, polite, formal.

She'd expected him to find some excuse to stay away. He didn't. 'Claibourne & Farraday is my primary concern at the moment. Unless you think India is ready to concede?'

'Not a chance,' she said, taking his cue, slowly shifting their relationship back to business. Where it should have stayed. Something they'd both forgotten in the supercharged atmosphere of grief and remembrance. 'It's just pride and stubbornness on your part,' she continued, with false brightness. 'Refusing to leave things the way they are.'

'Is that why you came here tonight? To tell me that?'

'No,' she said. 'You were right the first time. I expected to find you drowning your sorrows.'

'And were you rushing to my rescue, or were you planning to push me under?'

'That would be telling.'

Step by step they cranked their relationship back from the brink, sparring as if nothing was altered. As if the world hadn't just turned upside down for both of them. Then he ruined it all by saying, 'Just so you'll know for the future, Romana, I'll confess to having tried it twice. I discovered two things. One is that sorrow floats.'

'And the other?'

'That you feel like hell for days afterwards.'

'Wouldn't once have been enough to show you that?'

He favoured her with one of those ironical, self-deprecating smiles that he did to perfection. 'I was just checking to be sure.'

'You're a thorough man,' she said, and reached up to touch his cheek, where she'd kissed away his tears. It was the first time she'd seen a man cry. She hadn't known they were capable of such emotion. She had no experience of it. 'Will you be all right on your own?'

'And if I say no?' She frowned. 'Would you stay?'

She hesitated a moment too long before she said, 'That was a one-off, Niall. An inevitable response to an excess of emotion. A repeat performance would be self-indulgence. Or possibly a cynical ploy by me to undermine your position.' She offered him the chance to blame her for what had happened, ease his guilt. 'You'd never know.'

'I don't believe you've got a cynical bone in your body,' he said, rejecting her sacrifice.

If she hadn't already made the mistake of falling in love with him, she would have done so then. But falling in love with the enemy was only ever going to leave her exposed on all sides. With no one to turn to for comfort when it all ended in tears. And this time she'd be the one shedding them.

'What about you?' she asked. 'How cynical are you?'

She already knew the answer. A cynical man wouldn't have got the name wrong. He wouldn't have been that lost in desire. And he clearly thought her question beneath answering. Maybe that was why he slotted a CD into the Aston's music system—why he chose music rather than conversation on the drive across London.

She couldn't wait to escape, clambering out of the car before he could help her. But he insisted on walking her up to her front door, waiting while she unlocked it, his hand lightly on her arm, detaining her when she would have turned to shut the door.

'Romana...' he began. And then couldn't find the words.

'Don't! Please don't apologise. There's no need. You love Louise. You haven't come to terms with her death.' Then, as he turned to go, she was the one with her hand on his arm. 'Niall—' He waited. 'You probably don't want to hear this...' But she was going to say it anyway. 'You'll honour Louise most by living your own life well. She wouldn't want you to waste it in self-pity, or regret. In her place...' She stopped. That was never going to happen. 'If she loved you—'

'If?' he repeated.

'If she loved you as much as you love her—'

But whatever he'd been going to say she'd jerked him out of it, and he wasn't listening.

'For a girl whose mother abandoned her for a fat pay-off, whose father thinks a chequebook is the answer to everything, you seem to know a hell of a lot about love.'

'That's old news,' she said, and shivered.

'It was new to me.'

She looked up. He'd been listening to all that rubbish she'd poured out?

'When did you last see her?' he asked.

She raised an eyebrow.

'Oh, I see. I must live well. You can wallow in self-pity. Well, if you want my opinion, Romana—'

'I don't.'

'—I believe your mother was the loser.'

She swallowed back her own tears. 'You don't know what you're talking about.' Her mother had soon made up her loss with other babies. Little titled babies.

'As for Peter Claibourne, he's a man with a pride problem. A man who knows the price of everything and the value of nothing. Beautiful women. His children. Possession is all. He's never learned to cherish the objects of his desire.'

'He loves India.' The words were out before she'd thought them. But then they'd always been there, buried in her subconscious. Stirring up someone else's dark memories, she discovered, could backfire. 'Forget I said that. Please. He loves us all…'

'Love is such a catch-all word, with so many shades of meaning. It involves a lot more than woolly sentiment. If your father had taken the trouble to get to know you, build a relationship, he'd never have bought you that car for your seventeenth birthday.'

'You don't know what you're talking about.'

'Don't I? Isn't that why you gave it away? Not as some fine altruistic gesture but in a fit of girlish pique.'

'You—'

His fingers flew to her lips, blocking the expletive. 'You know I'm right. And if he loved India, really loved her, he wouldn't have left her with the mess she's in now. Think about it.' Then, after the slightest hesitation, he bent and kissed her cheek. 'I'll see you tomorrow, Romana.'

'Not if I see you first!'

She shut the door on him. Double-locked it, slid the bolt into place, and with her hand over her mouth, still warm from his touch, leaned back against the door. Then, stripping off her clothes, she flung herself into bed, repeating over and over to herself the word he'd blocked with his fingers.

It didn't wipe out the heat of his touch. Or the painful longing to be held that way again. The longing to have him make her believe she was cherished, cared for. Just for a minute. Just so that she'd know how it felt.

Then, because it was a weakness that she refused to submit to, she got up and splashed her face with cold water.

She would not love him, she told herself over and over again. She would not love any-one.

Niall, the wreckage of his life strewn across the kitchen floor, sat for a long time in the dark, thinking about Romana Claibourne. About how she'd broken through the barriers he'd erected to protect himself from feeling anything ever again. How he'd held her, kissed her, made love to her right here on Louise's sofa.

Except it wasn't Louise's sofa. His wife had been dead for four years. And he had been dead, too, in every way that was important. Until Romana Claibourne, sexy, smart and with a smile that could light up the night, had dropped a carton of coffee at his feet.

From the first moment he'd set eyes on Romana she'd been impossible to ignore. He'd had all the opportunities in the world to walk away. There had never been any intention to spend all day and every day with her. Heaven alone knew how often she'd told him to go away. Yet he had stayed. Put pressing business of his own on hold.

He began to pick up the photographs, one by one, looking at each of them for a long time before putting them back into the box. Putting the lid back in place. He would never forget

Louise, he knew. She would always be in his heart. But Romana was right. She had loved him. He would have changed places with her if he could. And if he had been the one who'd died, she would have felt the same way.

That was what love was.

But nothing could change what had happened. No amount of guilt, no amount of self-imposed suffering would bring her back. And tonight, looking at the photographs of their wedding, he had finally accepted that. That Romana had seen it so clearly, had finally used words that Louise might have used in the same situation, had hurt. But only because she was right. Living well was exactly what Louise would have expected from him.

He'd cried out her name tonight, but it hadn't been some attempt to fool himself that the woman in his arms was Louise. It had been goodbye. He just hadn't understood.

Romana had released him from a self-imposed prison and unwittingly he'd hurt her. Saying sorry would never be enough. He had to do something, show her how much he cared.

And he opened the cuttings file provided by Jordan and began to search for something…anything that might give a clue.

'On your own? No faithful shadow?' Romana looked up as India stopped by her office door. Then, 'You look terrible, Ro. Was there a party after the show last night?'

'I've no idea. I left as soon as it was over.'

'I hear Niall Macaulay didn't waste much time on the fashion show, either.' Her sister's voice rose on a probing little suggestion that maybe they'd been together.

'Really?' Romana asked. 'You heard that? I didn't know Molly was keeping you up to date with all the gossip.'

'She didn't volunteer the information, believe me. It took thumbscrews. But since you don't seem to think it's necessary to keep me up to date—'

'There's nothing to tell. I was tired and Niall had to be somewhere else. And so do you. You're handing over the neonatal equipment today at the hospital. Had you forgotten?'

'I'm on my way. Can I give you a lift?'

'No. Everything's organised. Molly can manage without me.' She picked up her bag. 'I'll be along in time for the lunch.'

'Romana…'

She waited. Her sister crossed the office and picked up the mobile phone lying on her desk.

'Don't forget this,' she said, switching it on. 'I need to be able to talk to you at any time.'

Romana realised, belatedly, that India didn't look all that hot either. Her sister's problems with the store were greater than anything she had to deal with. 'Have you heard from Dad?' she asked.

'He's not answering my calls.'

No surprise there. Niall was right. Their father had gone on an extended holiday to convalesce, leaving them to deal with the Farradays while he drank cocktails and flirted with pretty women who recognised a good thing when they saw it. 'We're on our own, then.'

'Men! Who needs them?' India grinned. 'Although from what Molly's been telling me, you and Niall Macaulay are striking sparks off one another. Maybe you should put personal prejudice on the back-burner and think of the store. If you seduced him, it would utterly compromise him.'

Romana felt the betraying heat rise to her face as she said, 'Molly doesn't know what she's talking about.'

'Really? And yet you always speak so highly of her when you're twisting my arm to raise her salary. Didn't he take you out to lunch yesterday?'

'You girls *have* had a nice chat.'

'Well?'

'We had lunch,' she admitted, and was finally able to grin back. 'A cheeseburger and fries with a large diet cola at the drive-thru by the roundabout.'

'Right. I guess I'll save the seduction plan for Flora, then. It's time she pulled her weight.'

'Lucky Flora,' Romana said, drily. 'And how do *you* propose to go about bringing Jordan Farraday to his knees?'

'I've got my moles digging for dirt. There must be some.'

'Watch yourself. They've got press cuttings on us from birth.'

They must have if the one in her bag was anything to judge by. An envelope had been lying on her doormat when she'd dragged herself from bed at the insistent ringing of the alarm. She'd opened it and found a magazine article about her mother. The small note attached said, 'Nothing is ever as simple as it appears from the outside. Ask her to tell you her story. Niall.'

Romana didn't phone first. She'd used to do that when she was a teenager—ring her mother's number, hoping to hear her voice. But there had always been someone else to answer the telephone. An au pair, or a housekeeper. And if her mother had answered she'd have hung up anyway. Because what was there to say?

She stepped out of the taxi and looked up at the elegant town house as she paused for a moment to take a deep breath, steady her pounding heart. Then she walked up the path and knocked on the front door.

It was opened by a tall, tanned young woman, with a child of perhaps six or seven clutching at her legs. She smiled shyly up at Romana, then coughed.

'Bless her, she's got a cold,' said the au pair, an Australian whose warm voice was full of laughter as she scooped the child up and hugged her.

'Who is it, Charlie?' a voice called from a room at the rear of the house.

'I'm Romana Claibourne,' she told the girl, handing her the magazine clipping. 'Will you please give this to Lady Mackie and ask her if she'll see me?'

'Charlie?' Romana's mother appeared at the end of the hall. Her stunning figure had thickened a little with the years and the babies, and tiny lines plucked at the corners of her eyes, but she was still a great beauty. She always would be. And in the flesh her face had a warmth that the glamorous photographs

Romana had cut out of magazines as a child and a teenager, and hidden away in a shoebox at the bottom of her wardrobe, had never captured.

Then she'd got older and realised her romantic fantasies about why her mother had left her were so much nonsense, had stopped listening to that tiny hopeful voice that had reasoned that one day—one day—she'd come. She'd stopped reading the stories. Stopped looking at the pictures. Made a little funeral pyre of the shoebox fantasies and let it all go.

But Niall was suggesting there was another side to the story. Prodding her as she'd prodded him.

For a moment her mother stared against the light, her eyes narrowing as she sought to recognise her caller.

'It's Romana Claibourne,' the au pair said, handing her the cutting before taking the child upstairs.

'Romana?' The voice was soft and husky. Familiar and yet strange. 'Romana, is it really you?'

Romana fought the pull, the emotional need. 'Someone—a friend—gave me that cutting and I had to know if it was true. What you said. About making mistakes. Do you really regret—?'

But her mother didn't wait for her to finish. She reached out, took her hands. 'Oh, my dear, dear child. I'd almost given up hoping. I thought you'd never come.'

CHAPTER ELEVEN

'How's it going?' Romana looked around, trying to spot Niall in the crowd, listening to India giving her short speech. 'Where's Niall?'

Molly raised her eyebrows. 'I assumed he was with you.'

'But I…' She stopped. Niall had anticipated that she'd go and see her mother and had given the hospital a miss in order to catch up on his own affairs. 'I'll see you later.'

'But what about this lunch? There'll be a gap at the table. Who's the Honourable Whatsit going to sit next to?'

'You're my deputy. Deputise!'

Outside the hospital, she was able to use her mobile phone to call Niall's office. His secretary appeared to be expecting her call and told her that Niall was away from the office for a few days.

She called him on his mobile. All she got was his voice, asking her to leave a message. But a message wouldn't do. Some things were too important for a message.

Last night she couldn't have imagined any circumstance under which she would return to his house in Spitalfields. But this morning...this morning anything might be possible.

She hailed a black cab and gave the driver his address.

The taxi seemed to crawl through the midday traffic. She would have been faster on her bike. But it gave her time to think. Think about him going home last night to an empty house, those poignant photographs. Instead of cursing her for pushing him to confront his grief he'd set about searching out a magazine article— one that described her mother's involvement in a charity working with the children of divorced couples. In it she'd spoken so sadly of mistakes that she'd made, her regret that her own daughter was lost to her.

It had been pushed through her letterbox some time during the night. He'd crossed

London with it, wanting her to know the truth. Wanting to give her back something she'd thought lost for ever. And he had succeeded, while she'd only given him pain.

She paid off the cab and climbed the short flight of steps to the door. Then, as she reached for the knocker, she momentarily lost her nerve.

How would he look? What would he say? Maybe he wouldn't want her to come in.

More importantly, what was *she* going to say?

Thank you. She'd just say thank you... She sniffed... And he'd know... And then...

'Romana?'

She waved her hand impatiently at the interruption.

'Romana, why are you talking to yourself?'

'Because I have to get it right...' She swung around. *'Niall!'*

'You seem surprised to see me. Considering you're standing on my doorstep.'

'Yes, well...' She indicated the front door, then him... Then realised that she was making a complete fool of herself. 'I was about to knock.'

'And rehearsing what you'd say first?' He smiled. 'How did it come out?'

She lifted her shoulders in an awkward little shrug. 'I thought I'd start with a simple ''thank you'' and see how it went from there.' He was wearing a pair of old jeans and a T-shirt and they—and his arms and hair—were liberally splattered with white paint. He looked, she thought, wonderful. 'Thank you.'

'That's it?'

No, it was far from 'it'. She wanted to fling her arms about him and give him a very personal demonstration of 'thank you'. But suddenly she wasn't even sure she should be here. 'I have to get back to the office now.'

'Come and have some lunch first.' He put a can of paint and some brushes on the doorstep, along with a brown paper sack, and searched his pocket for a doorkey. 'Public Relations Directors eat lunch, don't they?'

'I should be at the hospital lunch right now. So should you. You should be there observing me being brilliant. Being unique. Being utterly irreplaceable.'

'I've already seen you in action. You have ticks in all the right boxes.' He should have been grinning, but he wasn't. 'Are you saying that you missed me?'

'Of course I didn't miss you!' Of all the arrogant… 'I wasn't even there.'

'Really? And the sky didn't fall in? Maybe I should revise those ticks.'

About to say that she wasn't under any illusion about being indispensable, she realised that such an admission would play right into his hands. Last night she'd ignored the fact that he was a Farraday. This morning she'd all but forgotten.

'I let Molly run the show. I had something more important to do.'

'Well, I'm sure she enjoyed having the chance to spread her wings, show what she can do,' he said, his arm at her back as he ushered her inside. 'She's bright and ambitious.'

'She's also married,' Romana snapped back. And then, horrified at having exposed this previously untapped vein of jealousy, she rushed on, 'If you do get the store, I'll take her with me.'

'You're admitting the possibility? Things are looking up.'

'I'm admitting nothing.'

'No? Well, I'm not going to argue with you. But you have to face the fact that Molly might not want to follow you into the wilderness.'

'You really think she'd work for you?' she demanded, turning and standing her ground.

'I might make her an offer she can't refuse,' he replied, shutting the door and backing her up the hall in the direction of the kitchen. 'I bet she'd really like to be head of her own department. And with you there that's never going to happen, is it? She'll always be your number two.'

How many days had he been shadowing her? And already he knew more about her assistant than she did. Was she taking Molly's loyalty for granted? Was she really that insensitive? She swallowed. 'Maybe,' she admitted.

'For certain. You might be sentimental about the Claibourne management style, but I promise you no one else will be. They'll all be too busy hanging onto their jobs. Come and tell me about your morning.'

'My morning?' She needed time to get used to what had happened that morning. 'What about yours? Does Jordan know that you played hooky?' she demanded.

'Jordan doesn't own me. Besides, I already know everything that matters about you.' He reached out and took her hand to stop her from backing away from him, and kept walking until she had nowhere left to go.

'Oh, really?' She sounded a little nervous, he thought. Maybe she was right to be nervous. Her candy-pink mouth was a wicked temptation to any man.

And she still owed him. Last night had been personal. The kiss was something else. To be collected at his leisure. And as publicly as possible. A debt of honour.

'And I asked first,' he insisted. 'You know where the kitchen is.'

'Look, I came to say thank you. I've done that…'

'Do it again,' he said and, with his arm about her waist to ensure she couldn't escape, he kissed her, just long enough to feel her resistance crumble. Then he stopped. A candy-pink mouth, baby-blue eyes and a neck that was beginning to haunt his dreams. He was beginning to fantasise about her neck. He stopped, waiting for the guilt to kick in. It didn't. It was as if he'd thrown off some great weight. But he hadn't. Romana had taken it from him. 'You really shouldn't have had your hair cut,' he said. 'I could have resisted you with that awful hair.'

'Right,' she said, briskly, 'a little of that kind of compliment goes a long way. And now I've said everything I came to say—'

He tightened his hold on her waist. 'The kitchen, Romana. You're not going anywhere until you've told me all about your morning. Did you see her?'

On the point of asking Who? in the same defensive stance that she'd always used when asked about her mother, she stopped herself. She no longer needed to feel defensive and she had Niall to thank for that. Without him she would never have known the truth.

'Yes,' she said. 'I saw her.'

'And?'

'We talked. She told me things.' She took the bag from him. 'This smells good. What is it?'

He let her go now that he knew she'd stay for a while. 'Some *mezze* from a Lebanese restaurant on the other side of the market. Sit down and I'll get some plates.'

'No, really—I have to get back… We've got a fund-raising lunch tomorrow.'

'Leave Molly to worry about it. The practice will be good for her. And you look tired.'

'Thanks.'

'It was a comment, Romana, not a criticism. You'd still turn heads if you were walking down the street.'

On the point of collapsing onto the sofa, she hesitated, then pulled out a wooden chair and sat at the table.

'Just stay away from take-away coffee-cartons and you'll be fine.'

'You're never going to forget that, are you?'

'No,' he said. 'It was a life-changing moment. You never forget those.'

He'd been having rather a lot of them lately. That moment she'd invited him to enjoy the scent he'd bought her. The way she'd straightened his tie. Her skin beneath his hand when he'd stopped her from digging a deeper and deeper hole with her runaway mouth. The way she'd looked with wet cotton clinging to her breasts, how it had felt with her legs wrapped around him, her voice whimpering softly, begging for more…

'Did you know who I was?' she demanded. 'When I got out of that taxi?'

'No. I was expecting a sober-suited businesswoman with a lawyer in tow.'

'Wait until June,' she murmured.

'Of course if you'd been laden with C&F carriers, instead of designer bags, I might have twigged. Not that I'm criticising the result,' he assured her. 'The dress was stunning.'

'It was supposed to be understated.'

Heaven help him if she ever chose to make an impact. 'Try a sack next time,' he advised, and changed the subject before the rush of heat got out of hand. Next time he wanted her in bed. He wanted her there when he woke up.

Thoughts like that didn't help, so he fetched some plates and concentrated on their lunch. 'Tell me about your mother,' he pressed, pulling out the chair next to hers. Anything to stop thinking about the way she'd unbuttoned her shirt. Or the fact that he was close enough to reach out and unbutton the one she was wearing now. 'How was it? Meeting her?'

'We talked a lot. She said that my father lost interest in her within a year of their wedding.'

'Not a man given to long-term commitment?'

'No. I suppose we should be grateful that he stopped marrying his amours after number three,' she said. 'Apparently fidelity isn't his strong point. She put up with his affairs for as long as she could because of me. Then she met

James and discovered what love was all about.'

'So why didn't she take you with her?'

'My grandmother apparently had her investigated when she married Daddy, and somehow found out that she'd had an affair with an older man before they met. A public figure. They'd met at a party and she'd been totally infatuated, pursued him relentlessly, and of course he'd been flattered.'

'She was very lovely,' he said. Her daughter had the same bone structure, the same generous mouth. He could have lived with the hair if he'd had to. Without it, he was lost.

'And he was very lucky,' she said. 'His wife forgave him, the newspapers were too busy hounding some politician caught with his trousers down to get wind of it, and my mother retired from the scene—miserable, hurt, feeling rather stupid, very guilty at the damage she'd done and very conscious of how much worse it could have been.'

'And your father picked up the pieces?'

'I doubt he noticed how vulnerable she was. Just how lovely. They both got what they wanted from it for as long as it lasted. She said that Daddy didn't make a fuss when she wanted out.'

'But your grandmother wasn't as kind?'

'My grandmother didn't care about my mother. She only cared about keeping custody of me. She threatened to send details of the affair to the newspapers unless she left me behind. The man involved is very special, Niall. He'd made one stupid mistake and my mother blamed herself entirely for that.'

'A little harsh.'

'Maybe. But she wasn't prepared to ruin him.'

'So she got her quickie divorce and a cash settlement to ease her pain, courtesy of Grandmama.'

'The money was nothing to do with it, but that's the way it looked. Everyone thought she took the money and ran. Compared with Daddy James wasn't rich, but he certainly wasn't a pauper. No one cared about that. The gossip was much more entertaining.'

'She could have demanded access.'

'No. That was the deal. Walk away. Don't look back. And she felt it was her punishment. She'd been bad; she didn't deserve me. She just hoped that one day I'd come and ask her why she'd done it, so that she could tell me everything. In the meantime she devoted herself to her husband and her family, worked hard for charitable causes.'

'Living well in the hope of a day like today?'

'There's been so much wasted time, and without that magazine cutting I'd never have made the first move. And you crossed London in the middle of the night to bring it to me.' She reached out, shyly touched his hand. 'I'll always be grateful.'

'Last night you made me see how much time *I've* wasted. It made me think about the years that you and your mother had missed. I had this feeling…something at the back of my mind…maybe something my father once said… It doesn't matter. I just thought I might find something if I looked in the cuttings.' He covered her hand with his own. 'It was that kind of night. Time to tidy up, put things in order, say goodbye. I have you to thank for making me face it.'

'You're welcome.'

'You'll get your reward.'

'Niall, I don't want...' She was lying. She wanted him so much that it hurt. 'This isn't anything to do with Claibourne & Farraday.'

'I know. That's something else entirely.' Then, 'It wasn't the middle of the night, though. It was dawn before I put that envelope through your door. I considered knocking, waking you up and inviting myself in for breakfast.'

'Why didn't you?'

Because it hadn't been breakfast he wanted. Because it had been too soon, too complicated. Because he had fences to mend before they could ever share breakfast. He didn't tell her that. Instead he said, 'Look in a mirror. Anyone with half an eye can see you need all the beauty sleep you can get.'

'Yeah, right. And I'm dying of hunger too. Are we going to get lunch, or what?' He shared his lunch between two plates. 'What is this?'

'Tabbouleh, humous, stuffed vine leaves, grilled vegetables,' he said, pointing to each in turn with his fork. Then he scooped up some stuff and offered it to her. 'Try this. It's called *Imam beyeldi*…''the Imam fainted''…' She tried it. 'Good?'

'Very good. Though whether I'd faint…' She waggled her hand back and forth to indicate that it was in doubt.

He tore a pitta bread in two and handed half to her. 'He apparently fainted over the cost of the olive oil involved in making it.'

'Oh, well, a man after your own heart, then,' she said. And immediately wished she hadn't. But he smiled, apparently taking it as the joke she had meant it to be. For a while they ate in companionable silence. Then Romana said, 'You haven't told me about your morning.' She reached out, touched the streak of paint on the back of his hand. 'You've been painting?'

'The ceiling in the drawing room upstairs. It's stupid, really, I can't possibly do it all. It's a gesture. A commitment.'

'To what?'

'To the future. To moving on. You said I should get out of here and I thought perhaps you might be right.'

'A first, then.'

'You talked a lot of sense last night and I did think about it. Seriously. I considered a Docklands apartment—all pale wood and brushed-steel minimalist. Or a mews cottage in Chelsea. Somewhere just to please myself, without the burden of history to live up to. The trouble was I couldn't see myself in any of them. For years I've camped out here, refusing to make it into a proper home because Louise isn't here to share it. But in spite of my neglect it is my home, and it's where I want to stay.'

'With the ghosts?'

'There are no ghosts here, Romana. Only me.'

'You and the very latest thing in eighteenth-century interior decoration.'

'No. I meant it about moving on. I thought I'd keep to the spirit of the age, though. Pale yellow with hand-painted ivy swags?' he suggested. 'I'll get a couple of students from the local art college in and let them loose.'

'It sounds charming,' she said, picturing the room drenched in sunlight rather than lurking in shadow. 'You'll keep the painted panelling in the hall, though?'

'You like it?'

'Does it matter what I like?'

'You like it?' he repeated.

'Yes, I like it.'

'Then it stays.'

'Great.' Romana had the disconcerting feeling that something had just happened and she'd missed it. 'Well, I really do have to be going.'

'I hoped you might volunteer to stay and help with the decorating.'

'Really?' It was hard to keep her racketing heart from running away with her mouth when staying and spending the day with him was such an appealing idea. But this was something he had to do on his own. 'Why would I want to do that?'

'For fun?'

'When I want fun,' she replied, 'I'll go shopping. I'll ask our interior design team to come and give you a quote, if you like. The whole works. Heating, plumbing, decoration.'

'I'd get a better rate if I waited until we take over.'

'Get real, Niall. It isn't going to happen. Beneath that stern exterior you're pure mush. You wouldn't take the store away from me.'

'Wouldn't I? And even if that were true, there's still Bram and Jordan. They're about as mushy as concrete.'

'They have to shadow Flora and India,' she countered. 'Ice and steel respectively,' she assured him. 'But thanks for lunch; it was a treat.'

'We're getting better at it,' he said. She looked up. 'The food thing. Maybe we could risk a restaurant next time?'

'Don't let's get ambitious.'

'You want to take it in easy stages? Okay, I'll give the formal lunch a miss tomorrow—'

No! That wasn't what she wanted to hear! 'I've got some stuff I have to clear up. Let's see how we manage at the ball on Saturday night. Who knows? We might even manage dessert.'

'Buffets are tricky things. The scope for disaster is legion.'

'I'm prepared to take the risk,' he said. 'If you are.'

His eyes seemed to be saying a lot more than the words. Romana swallowed. 'You're still coming to the charity ball, then? I thought you said you'd learned everything there was to know about me.'

'I lied. I have no idea if you can dance. Save something slow for me.'

'You dance?'

'That might be an exaggeration. I need someone to hold on to.'

'Niall...' He waited. 'Nothing. I'll make sure Molly's got you on the seating plan, shadow-man.'

'Don't forget that a shadow has to be...' he reached out and brushed his fingers against her throat '...touching close.'

CHAPTER TWELVE

ROMANA'S hair was a golden halo framing her face, balancing the elegant curve of her neck. And her dress was anything but understated. It was as insubstantial as gossamer: floating layers of black silk chiffon that drifted almost to her ankles but didn't hide them—or the exquisite shoes she was wearing. It was scattered with tiny black jet beads that caught the light as she moved. She wore a jet choker about her throat.

Not that anyone would be noticing her hair, or the dress. They wouldn't be able to tear their eyes from the plunging neckline.

'Niall…' He'd rapped on her apartment door, and when she'd opened it, her bag in her hand, her wrap over her arm, she'd for once been too surprised to say anything except his name. It had come out in a little rush of breath. 'What are you doing here?'

Losing his head.

Burning his boats.

Or did he mean jumping ship?

'I've come to take you to the ball, Cinders,' he said, his own breath taking a holiday. 'Your pumpkin awaits.'

'Niall, this is kind—'

She lied. She didn't think he was kind. She thought he had an ulterior motive and she was right. He hadn't seen her for two whole days and he wanted to be alone with her. To spend ten quiet minutes in her company before the mayhem of the evening. Just to sit beside her in the dark and hold her hand.

'—but I've got a car booked.' She glanced at the tiny jewelled wrist-watch that had replaced her workmanlike Rolex. As she lifted her wrist he caught the familiar scent of her perfume. Summer Shadow. Summer, autumn, winter, spring... 'It should be here any minute.'

'It is here. I told Molly to cancel your hire car. It seemed wasteful to have two when we're both going to the same place.'

Her flush darkened. 'Told her? You're not running Claibourne & Farraday yet.'

'Maybe you should be telling her that.'

'And you are certainly not my idea of a fairy godmother—'

'No? You don't know how glad I am to hear you say so. And on reflection I believe I may have got the wrong fairy tale.' This was more like a variation on *Sleeping Beauty*—only in this case Beauty had woken *him* with a kiss. He grinned. 'Cinderella would never have been allowed out in a dress like that.'

'You don't like it?'

'I didn't say that. I just hope you weren't trying for understated—because I'm telling you, you've failed. Totally.' And he took the wrap she was holding.

Romana couldn't stop a little smile tucking up the corners of her mouth as she turned to let Niall drape the soft fabric over her shoulders. 'No one goes for understated at a full-dress ball, Niall. *Celebrity* magazine wants its readers to be able to drool over the frocks.

What do you think?' she asked, turning to face him.

'I think…' She'd given him a chance to make some crass remark, but the sudden telling heat from his eyes almost burned her. The longer he thought about it, the more she really, really wished she hadn't asked such a stupid question. 'I think you should be locked up before you cause a riot,' he said. 'But maybe I'm easily impressed.'

She knew that wasn't true. But she'd won him round. He'd agreed when she'd said she was unique, brilliant, utterly irreplaceable. For a man so difficult to impress such an admission was pure gold. Suddenly charged with energy, confidence and feeling totally in control, she reached up and twitched his tie into line.

'Shall we go?' he said, taking her hand.

They sat in the back of the car, not quite touching. Only his hand over hers, never once letting go, connecting them.

'How's the decorating going?'

'The drawing room is finished.' He glanced at her. 'I got impatient and hired some help.'

'What next?'

'The kitchen needs some work.'

'Nothing too modern, though. You'll keep the butler's sink and the table and the dresser...?' She stopped.

'They're staying. The men start work tomorrow.'

'That's going to be tough to live with.'

'I thought I might go away for a while.'

'Oh.' Suddenly she didn't feel quite so on top of the world. 'Good decision,' she said.

'I'm long overdue a holiday.'

'Right.'

The car came to halt, but he didn't move his hand from hers even when the hotel doorman opened the car door. Didn't let go, didn't move. 'Save the first dance for me,' he said.

'The first dance?' They weren't the words any girl wanted to hear, and Romana's heart dipped a little further. 'I won't have time for dancing,' she said. 'Maybe I'll manage a few minutes later on.'

'There won't be a later.'

He wasn't staying? As she made a move his hand fastened over hers. 'The first dance,' he insisted and, taking her agreement as read, stepped out of the car—her hand still in his as he helped her out, his arm beneath her elbow as they entered the ballroom.

Romana immediately went into a huddle with Molly over last-minute changes to the running order of the evening. Niall had details of own to attend to and, having changed the seating arrangements so that he was beside Romana, he went in search of the master of ceremonies for the evening.

'You are so predictable, Niall Macaulay,' Romana said when, having toured the room with India and Flora, greeting friends, thanking contributors to the charity, she joined him at her table.

'Then you should have put me here in the first place.'

'You could have seen me from over there,' she protested.

'I could have seen you, but I couldn't have heard you, or...' he leaned closer so that he had a breathtaking view of her enticing cleavage '...enjoyed the delightful scent you're wearing.'

'It's new. I'm promoting it,' she reminded him.

'You've sold me. Shall we dance?' She glanced at the dance floor. It was empty. 'Someone has to make the first move,' he prompted.

'It should be India,' she hedged.

'She's busy winning friends and influencing people.'

'You're up to something,' she said, as he took her chair and she stood up.

'Of course I am.' He glanced at the MC who, primed with folding money, had been watching for his move and now approached the microphone.

As they reached the centre of the floor the MC said, 'My lords, ladies and gentlemen, please welcome Miss Romana Claibourne and Mr Niall Farraday Macaulay—members of the two great families who founded Claibourne & Farraday—who have gallantly volunteered to open the ball with a waltz.' There was a ripple of applause, a few whistles. 'But first Mr Macaulay is going to claim a special lot he bid for at the Claibourne & Farraday charity auction this week. A kiss from the lovely Miss Claibourne.'

Romana couldn't believe it. She'd thought they were beyond this. That if they could be nothing else they were friends. But he was going to throw it all away for a PR stunt. Just to show her that anything she could do, he could go one better.

And he was right. Nothing…*nothing*… would stop the editor of *Celebrity* from putting this picture on the cover.

It would probably make most of the morning newspapers too.

This was her field and he was upstaging her. Having agreed that she was unique, brilliant, he was now showing her that he was better, that he could make a front-page story that would wipe out everything she'd worked so hard to achieve.

He was a Farraday first and last, and even as she was trying to find the words to express her feelings he put his hand to her waist, drew her closer and for a moment looked down into her face. He had won and there was nothing she could do to stop him from claiming his prize.

His kiss. The store.

Around them a slow handclap began, and Niall finally lowered his lips to hers.

It would have been awful under any circumstances. A slow, lingering kiss that just went on and on, with an audience of a thousand whooping and clapping guests. But that wasn't the worst of it.

The worst of it was that her lips were responding with a heat she couldn't disguise. She was betraying her true feelings, every tender desire, as she kissed him back. She never wanted it to end. Because after it had ended there would be nothing.

But at last it was over. All her hopes, all her longings. Gone. Blown away. And the tears that welled up, spilled down her cheeks, left her with nothing. Not even her self-respect.

As the music began the ballroom and the crowds all faded away. They danced because they were supposed to dance. She felt so brittle she was sure she would break in his arms. But people didn't break. Hearts didn't break. They just felt that way.

Niall had finally shown his true colours.

For a few sweet moments she'd basked in what she'd thought might—just might—grow into something special.

She should have known better. The man was a Farraday. His heart might be broken, but he wouldn't let that get in the way of a business deal.

He stopped. The music was still playing but he'd stopped dancing, and she looked up, met his gaze head-on. 'Is that it?' she demanded. 'You've had enough? Did you get full value for your money this time?'

'That was just a down payment, Romana.'

'Oh, no. One PR stunt per night...'

'PR stunt? That wasn't a PR stunt, Romana. It was a public statement of intent. A statement to every Claibourne & Farraday in the world that I will not allow some stupid feud to keep us apart. A very public signal of a merger between you, Romana Elizabeth Claibourne, and me, Niall Farraday Macaulay, and a personal guarantee that Louise is in the past—where she belongs. She's a beloved memory, but not one that will ever come between us again.'

Romana heard the subtext. His regret that he had hurt her. His promise that it would never happen again. 'I love you, Romana, and I'm telling you now that I plan to go on claiming interest on that kiss for the next fifty years.'

'Fifty years?' She blinked back the tears that were now more determined than ever to overflow.

'If you'll have me.'

'But—but you hardly know me.'

'I know everything I need to know. And I recognise the real thing when I feel it.' He touched her face, brushed away a tear with the pad of his thumb. 'You are my fairy tale princess, waking me from a death-like sleep. And you know how all fairy stories end, don't you?'

The music had stopped. Around them the crowds stilled expectantly, unable to hear but aware that something momentous was happening.

'I'm offering you my heart, Romana. Will you take it?'

For a terrible moment she'd doubted him. But she would never doubt him again. She'd seen beneath the surface, past the hard-eyed businessman to the man. She'd seen his eyes as he'd wiped mayonnaise from her face. And when he'd kissed her before the auction he'd meant it...or why would he have been so angry with her for misunderstanding? He'd spent the night looking through old press cuttings to find out the truth about her mother, driven across town with the cutting. He hadn't had to do that.

When they'd made love he'd come to release with the name of his dead wife on his
lips. But as he'd made love to her, kissed her,
caressed her, taken care to ensure her pleasure
every step of the way, it had been *her* name
he was saying. Her name.

'Yes,' she said. 'Yes, please.' And as their
lips touched once more the only sound was the
sigh that rippled through the crowd.

Then he said, 'One more thing. I want you
to know that my surrender is total. Heart, body
and—'

'Soul?'

'Department store.'

She laughed. 'That sounded like a...
Elizabeth? How do you know my middle name
is Elizabeth?'

'I've been doing my homework. I wanted
you to be sure—as I am—that I have the right
woman. And I want you to know that whatever
decision is made about the future of
Claibourne & Farraday my voting share is at
your disposal. I'm trusting you to make the
right choice. As I'm trusting you with my life.'

They were centre stage, the object of specu-lation for a thousand pairs of eyes.

'Is that everything?' he asked. 'Or do you want me on my knees?'

'You'd do that?'

'If you insist.'

For a moment she pretended that she was seriously considering it. Then she laughed. 'Later. We'll save that until we're on our own.' And she grabbed his hand and headed for the exit.

'But what about all this?' he said, as there was a sudden burst of noise behind them.

She glanced back, saw India headed in their direction. 'Molly can handle it,' she said.

'We did the right thing.'

'I couldn't agree more.'

Romana lifted her hand so that she could see the wedding ring glinting on her hand in the moonlight. Niall reached up and laced his fin-gers through hers before pushing her down amongst the pillows to demonstrate just how right it was...

Later…much later…she said, 'If we'd told everyone first they'd have expected a huge family wedding.'

'You're right,' Niall conceded.

'I mean, it would have given the Claibourne & Farraday wedding department a PR spin that money couldn't buy, but I didn't want our wedding to be a PR event.'

'And a big family wedding might have been a little bit tricky under the present circumstances,' he added.

'But we're going to have to tell them,' she said.

'Go home and face the music?'

'Eventually,' she conceded. 'But we should have a honeymoon first, don't you think?'

'I didn't know two people could have such perfect understanding,' he murmured. Their fingers caught, entwined. 'But they'll be wondering where we are.'

'Maybe we should send them an e-mail.'

'Oh, that's a great idea.'

'I'm full of them. And I've just had another one…'

*   *   *

'Okay.' Romana sat at the terminal at the internet café, her fingers poised above the keyboard, the diamonds in her wedding ring flashing back the sun and Niall's arm about her waist. 'What shall we say?'

'Best keep it short and simple,' he advised. 'How about this? ''Just a note to let you both know that the shadowing was a complete success. Married yesterday. See you—eventually. Love, Romana and Niall.'''

MILLS & BOON® PUBLISH EIGHT LARGE PRINT TITLES A MONTH. THESE ARE THE EIGHT TITLES FOR SEPTEMBER 2002

❦

THE WEDDING ULTIMATUM
Helen Bianchin

HER BABY SECRET
Kim Lawrence

SWEET SURRENDER
Catherine George

LAZARO'S REVENGE
Jane Porter

HIS MAJESTY'S MARRIAGE
Winters & Gordon

THE CORPORATE BRIDEGROOM
Liz Fielding

THE TYCOON'S TEMPTATION
Renee Roszel

THEIR DOORSTEP BABY
Barbara Hannay

MILLS & BOON®

0802 Rom LP

MILLS & BOON® PUBLISH EIGHT LARGE PRINT TITLES A MONTH. THESE ARE THE EIGHT TITLES FOR OCTOBER 2002

───────── ❦ ─────────

THE ARRANGED MARRIAGE
Emma Darcy

THE DISOBEDIENT MISTRESS
Lynne Graham

THE GREEK TYCOON'S REVENGE
Jacqueline Baird

THE MARRIAGE PROPOSITION
Sara Craven

THE PRINCE'S PROPOSAL
Sophie Weston

THE MARRIAGE MERGER
Liz Fielding

THE BABY DILEMMA
Rebecca Winters

THE PREGNANCY PLAN
Grace Green

MILLS & BOON®

0902 Rom